Shazaf Fatima Haider is the author of *How It Happened*. She is currently a full-time mother and part-time writer and dearly wishes she had a nanny to make it the other way round. *A Firefly in the Dark* is her second novel.

I0649525

A Firefly in the Dark

Shazaf Fatima Haider

talking
CUB

TALKING CUB

Published by Speaking Tiger Publishing Pvt. Ltd
4381/4, Ansari Road, Daryaganj
New Delhi 110002

Published in India in Talking Cub by Speaking Tiger
in paperback in 2018

ISBN: 978-93-87693-54-8
eISBN: 978-93-87693-33-3

10 9 8 7 6 5 4 3 2 1

For sale in South Asia only

Typeset in Garamond Premier Pro by SÜRYA, New Delhi

Printed at Sanat Printers, Kundli

For the readers—
both invisible and visible.

Chapter 1

There was a reason Sharmeen's mum had forbidden her from listening to Nani's stories. No cuddly creatures scampered about getting into merry scrapes and happy endings here. Dark Ones lurked in these tales: furious snake-women avenged their dead offspring through fangs and poison; witches with mangled feet bit off the heads of piglets and cast black spells to lure unsuspecting victims into dark forests from which they never emerged. Tonight, Nani narrated the gruesome story of Samarkand, the unfortunate traveller, while her twelve-year-old granddaughter lay curled up against her, wide-eyed and trembling.

'His feet ached. The sun descended into the violet mountains in the west, highlighting the silhouette of a black willow tree in the distance. Wreathes of old leaves dangled from its branches, reminding Samarkand of his mother's untied hair as she begged him not to leave home. But he was not content being a lowly woodcutter. He wanted more than a lifetime of felling beautiful trees. So under the cold shade of the dark willow he lay, leaning against the rotting bark. He drifted into a deep slumber, but little did he know...'

The last words made Sharmeen scoot closer to her grandmother. This was the point of dramatic irony: where she would know something Samarkand did not. Nani shifted, making room on the bed, lazily gazing into the distance where visions of verdant fields, thick-leaved willows and sleeping sons swirled.

'Little did he know that the willow was the special abode of a Janeeree: a cruel she-Jinn who lived within the cocooned spirals of the tree's dead leaves. As Samarkand snored, the Janeeree awoke. She drew the drooping curtains aside and scuttled down the thin branches. Her amber eyes spotted her sleeping prey, oblivious to the danger looming above him. Licking her lips with a forked tongue, she made her way further down. She was a fierce creature with sharp, sabre-like teeth unfolding from the grooves of her mouth as she neared. Below her waist, eight spidery legs, slender and bent, moved slowly and steadily towards Samarkand's body.'

Nani looked down at her button-nosed granddaughter whose lips quivered with anticipation and barely suppressed questions. 'But the truth is that when Jinn are around, nothing is inevitable. Just when the mouth is open and the fangs are drawn, something unexpected happens.'

'A twist!' Sharmeen proclaimed triumphantly. Nani chuckled, her crinkled face unfurling into a wide grin, and carried on.

'The Janeeree crept on leg after naked leg, inching towards Samarkand's sleeping form. Her jaw unlocked like an anaconda's, preparing to swallow the sleeping man whole. But his smell made her stop.'

'Body odour?' Sharmeen enquired.

'Dhat!' snapped Nani, signalling amused disapproval. 'It was not body odour! He smelt of unshed tears. It was an unfamiliar wetness for her smokeless fire.'

'Smokeless fire, Nani?'

'Yes. Humans are made from clay, angels from air, and Jinn from smokeless fire.'

'How can fire be smokeless?'

'Because the first flame ever created by God was pure. It blazed and yet did not burn, sustaining without destroying: a beautiful lamp in the sky. From this, the earliest Jinn were born. Their breath formed the first suns around which planets would cluster. They adored their Master and did His bidding, their loyalty engendered by wonder, awe and fear.'

'They sound beautiful.'

'Oh, they were. They could cut through mountains the way a knife slices through butter. They breathed on galaxies, and their heat made the cold stars flow like liquid rivers in the sky. They fashioned many beautiful worlds, adorning the inky universe with glittering galaxies. Fiery artisans of the five skies: they began to admire their craft and gloat in its glory. Slowly, arrogance crept in, followed by rebellion. Who was God—they whispered among themselves—but a broken architect, closeted up in the seventh domain, distant and invisible? Did they not do His work for Him? Did *He* not need *them*? He was nothing but an old, decrepit Jinn, losing power, hiding His weaknesses from His children. So they rose up in dissent.'

'Did God punish them?'

'He let the consequences of their misdeeds taint them instead, hurling them out of Heaven, banishing them into the worlds they had constructed. When they gazed upon all they had lost, they wept with bitter regret, choking and gagging, their tears mingling with their fiery beings to create a black, acrid smoke that spread into our world. That is why our flames are hot, destructive; no longer eternal. Some Jinn strove to reclaim their purity through atonement. But others, like the Janeeree, forgot that they had ever been pure.'

'So they're not smokeless anymore?'

'They were made smokeless, but do not remain so. They thought, as the Janeeree did, that the smoke, like the evil inside them, was now a permanent part of their being. Thus it came to pass that the Janeeree adopted the path of the damned, walked by all who are disobedient.'

Sharmeen gulped. She was on the path of the damned right now; just yesterday she had promised her mother that she would no longer listen to Nani's Jinn stories.

'So Jinn are like flames in the air? Is that what they are?'

'No, my love. Jinn are a part of the invisible realm. We cannot see them, but they can see us. They are powerful enough to traverse the seen and unseen worlds. This planet has stones, plants, animals, humans, but it also has Jinn, and we all coexist. Now, may I continue my story?'

'Yes! Sorry.'

'Where was I?'

'The Janeeree was about to eat Samarkand, but was interrupted by his body odour.'

Nani sighed and shook her head. 'She bends her legs, all eight of them, and kneels. Slowly, she runs a long slender finger along his cheek. She has missed the feel of a man's beard. A creature of impulse, she decides not to kill Samarkand, because she is lonely.'

'Why lonely?'

'How many people do you think would befriend a Janeeree, whose bitter pastime consisted of ensnaring travellers who sought refuge underneath her tree? She liked to sniff out their fears and chant, giving them nightmares until they woke up, screaming in mindless terror. And when she tired of toying with them, she bled them, leaving their corpses rotting on the ground. But not this time. The Janeeree decided to use Samarkand by binding him to herself.'

'How?'

'Stop interrupting, child!' admonished Nani before continuing. 'The Janeeree put Samarkand's head on her lap and murmured prayers of the ancient realm, of days before the sun and stars, of swirling infernos and thick goop. She wove a heady spell of passion and whispered it into his ear. He dreamt of a beautiful woman, bereft and abandoned, reaching out to him through the dark halo of her hair.

'He awoke from a fitful sleep and saw the same woman, naked and trembling before him. He covered her with his caftan and offered her food, which she declined. Janeerees cannot partake of human food, you see. Women who never eat are often she-Jinn in disguise—waiting for men to go to sleep, feasting on human bones in the dead of night... but how was Samarkand to know all this? He was under the heady spell of love. He promised to rescue her, but she cried and said that she was tied to the tree by an evil sorcerer who had cast a curse on her. He would not let her go unless she conceived a child from the son of man.'

'I didn't know that Janeerees could trap men like that.'

'It is perfectly common. Many poets write about beautiful women calling out to them in their dreams, not knowing that they are in the thrall of Janeerees wanting to possess them.'

'But can Janeerees and men have children? Is that even possible? Wouldn't Samarkand get burnt—you know, because she was made of fire?'

'Only if she assumed her unbodied self. Janeerees are mistresses of disguise: as human women, they can touch men without harming them. So it came to pass: Samarkand vowed to help his damsel in distress. He built a small cottage next to the willow and decided to break the sorcerer's spell. And then, one day, his woman told him that she was carrying his child.

'Samarkand was jubilant! "Let us rid ourselves of this infernal tree of your prison." But the Janeeree laughed and revealed her fearful self: eight legs erupted from her protruding belly, and she bared her fangs at Samarkand, who, poor man, ran blindly into the glare of day, forgetting his love, his cottage, everything. But in the evening, he came back.'

'Why?'

'He could not leave behind the child that was his.'

'But he had abandoned his mother!'

'You are right. Samarkand had gone forth to search for adventure, but his quest had become his curse. He had left his mother's arms only to stumble into the selfish embrace of the Janeeree. She would taunt him with hoots of hollow laughter as he sat under the willow in quiet vigil, waiting for his child to be born. Months passed, and still he remained, tormented, guilty, but adamant. And one night, he heard blood-curdling screams of terror from above. He ran out from his cottage to see the Janeeree wrestling a fierce creature, with a scorpion's tail and an eagle's claws.'

'What was it?'

'A Labartu: a fire-demon that lives on the first breath of newborns. It sucks their life and is regenerated.'

'That's awful!'

'Yes, Labartus are vile creatures, burning with hunger. Such a one had sniffed the new infant in the Janeeree's womb and wished to scoop it out—for the fresher the foetus, the more potent the life force. It was stronger than the Janeeree and chased her from branch to branch. Samarkand was helpless as he watched the tangle of legs and limbs, now enmeshed, now separated, struggling furiously. When the Janeeree screamed for help, he ran back to his cottage and combed through his satchel for something, anything that could help her. All he found was a small string of silver prayer beads his mother had gifted to him. He ran outside, yelling to the Janeeree to come and take it. She swept down and put it around her neck just as the Labartu lunged at her. Samarkand saw it opening its black mouth over the Janeeree's womb, but it was yanked back by an invisible force. Again and again, the Labartu lashed out at the Janeeree, who cowered in the nook of two branches. But it could not reach her. The creature yowled in frustration. After one final swoop, it fell on the ground, slithered down a small burrow and disappeared.

'Samarkand heard the Janeeree sobbing. He began to climb the tree, but stopped when he heard another sound: a high-pitched squawk. Through the leaves, he saw her climbing down; a small human babe in her arms, its eyes the shade of a peacock's blue. The Janeeree put the beads around its neck and gave it to Samarkand. She repaid him for his help by negotiating a truce: at night, the child would remain cloistered in the willow with its mother; during the day, Samarkand could venture with him as far as he pleased, just so long as he could return to the tree in time.

'So Samarkand lived, tied to his son and the Janeeree, haunted by nightmares of his mother's woes. Years passed, and he grew old. One night, the Janeeree visited him, and she saw that the young, handsome man she had once claimed had become old and shrivelled, a shadow of his former dreams.

'Once again, something stirred in her heart. Not passion, not greed. For the first time, she felt pity. And she did to him what she would have the first night he came her way:

she sucked his breath into hers, waiting for the light in his eyes to go out. She left his body to become dust and floated away to a different tree.'

'What happened to the baby?'

'Born of Jinn and man, neither Jinn nor man, he was an Amluq. He wandered the world, searching for hidden knowledge. He is a spirit whispered about, a legend who makes himself visible to those who need his help, invisible to those who don't believe in stupid things like Jinn and Janeerees...End of story. That's enough for tonight. Now let me sleep.'

Sharmeen sat up and hugged her knees. 'You mean, Nani, that my mother won't be able to see him?'

'No. She doesn't believe in things that she cannot see.'

'Didn't you tell her these stories when she was my age?'

'Oh, I did tell her, but she was afraid and ran away from them. And now she's grown up, my love, and some grown-ups think that stories are only on paper. They do not like knowing that there are things that cannot be seen with the eye.'

'But Amma does believe in what she can't see. She believes in God.'

'Yes, I do, Sharmeen,' said Aliya, her voice making both grandmother and granddaughter jump, as unexpected sounds after Jinn stories are wont to. Sharmeen turned around to see her mother's tall, slim frame leaning against the doorway, her arms crossed and lips pursed in obvious displeasure.

'Amma, is this your idea of putting Sharmeen to sleep?'

'The child wanted a story, so I told her one!' said Nani, scowling.

'Right. And now Sharmeen will have nightmares till goodness knows when.'

'She will not. She is my granddaughter and knows that nightmares only come to a weak mind. We seek God's protection every night, don't we, Sharmeen?'

Sharmeen thought best not to answer—silence was a good strategy when one was caught between two bickering women. She scrambled off the bed. 'Good night, Nani! May the Angels protect you when you ascend tonight!'

Aliya rolled her eyes. 'Yes, Amma, happy *ascending*. Sharmeen, off to bed. Now.'

Sharmeen tried to hurry, but she tottered on one leg, slipping her foot into one of the dark green shoes that lay on the floor. The other seemed to have disappeared—she'd probably kicked it under the bed. She went down on her knees, reaching underneath, but to no avail.

'Hurry up, Sharmeen!' Aliya admonished.

'I'm trying!' she whined. Nani was muttering a prayer. Sharmeen peered at the slipper, reaching for it, the frame of the bed preventing her from reaching any further. But something odd happened: she saw—no, it couldn't be, but yes that's what happened—she saw the slipper *move* towards her as if something invisible were nudging it towards the palm of her hand. She froze and looked up at her grandmother, who winked mischievously. Grabbing the slipper and pulling it out, she ran out of the room, leaving her mother behind.

Aliya shot an irate glance at her mother. 'See? She's terrified already! Good night!'

Nani watched her daughter walk away and mimicked her parting words, gesticulating to the rocking chair in the corner that nobody sat on.

Chapter 2

Beds become like the people who sleep on them. A deep sleeper has a soft one, letting her sink comfortably into its shelter. The insomniac has bumps like fat thumbs poking at her back. Aliya lay on a large bed that was carved with a patterned trellis, its little crevices coated with dust. Nips and etches created a rugged design in the dark wood. Two hour-glass pillars stretched from the foot of the bed, making it solid, heavy and cumbersome. She stared at the ceiling, lost in her thoughts.

'Amma? Are you awake?'

Aliya turned and saw Sharmeen's head peeking at her from behind the bedpost.

'I am now, Sharmeen.'

'Well. I thought to check on you. To see whether you were scared.'

'That's very kind of you. I'm fine.'

'In any case, I think it best that I lie down with you to make sure you feel safe.'

'Sharmeen, *why* do you listen to Nani's stories if they scare you?'

'I'm not scared. Now make some space for me.'

Aliya sighed in resignation and turned on her side. Sharmeen squeezed close and Aliya hugged her, silently cursing her mother, who was sleeping in the room down the hallway.

'There are no Jinn here. Relax.'

'There could be some here, but you can't see them because you don't believe in them.'

Aliya rolled her eyes. 'Then you must also stop believing.'

'Nani says unbelievers don't have any imagination.'

'She may be right.'

'But she says they're real.'

'Be that as it may, have you ever thought about how you have existed safe and unharmed for so long? *If* Nani's stories are true, then an evil Jinn should have snatched you out of my arms when you were born, or strangled you in your sleep. But you're alive and well.'

'Because Jinn are only interested in women, not girls, and I have to wait for blood.'

'*What?*'

'Nani told me that when girls bleed, they become women.'

'Do you know what that means?'

'Yes. Nani told me everything. Or is that one of her stories too?'

'No, no. She's right about that. I was going to talk to you about it when you were a little older, but...'

'It's okay, Amma. I know about it all. But you know, Nani says that women will all go to heaven because they bleed: it's our penance on earth; therefore we need no penance in hell.'

'Beta, Nani is old and she babbles. She's beginning to believe that her stories are true. It happens to old people sometimes.'

Sharmeen thought about it for a moment, lying on her mother's uncomfortably bony arm; Aliya had lost a lot of weight in the past year. She shifted to find a comfortable angle and thought about her mother's assessment. Yes, Nani was a little mad at times, talking to herself, roaming the halls at midnight, combing her startlingly white hair only when the windows were closed. But she was strong—a forceful personality within a small frame that Sharmeen could lean on.

Snuggling closer against her mother, she sighed. Night was the only time when Amma belonged to her, undistracted by a headache or a to-do list.

'Amma, tell me about Abba.'

She felt Aliya stiffen.

'Baby, you know what happened to Abba.'

'Tell me again.'

'Why do you want to hear it?'

'Because you tell it well.'

'It's not make-believe, Sharmeen. It's true,' her mum said, drawing her close for a hug. Sharmeen rejoiced in its warmth, pitying poor Samarkand who had deliberately rejected this wonderful feeling of skin and snuggle for mere adventure.

But then they'd had their own share of adventure—if you could call it that. Her father's jeep had been hit by a truck on the highway six months ago. Both vehicles had been badly damaged; but Amir had emerged from the wreckage largely unhurt thanks to the fact that he always wore a seatbelt. The truck driver, however, had a nasty wound above his eye and her father had helped him out of his seat and wrapped a tie around his head before calling emergency services.

'Then Abba called you, right?'

'Yes.'

'What did he say?'

'He said he was fine.'

'And?'

'And he asked if you were okay. He'd had a vision of you while he was unconscious, that you were searching for him, chased by a cloud of black smoke just behind you. And then he'd seen you laughing and playing and dangling your legs, sitting on a tree while a glow-worm hovered above your hair.'

'Wasn't that a beautiful vision?'

'He was probably hallucinating, baby.'

'And then he told you he loved you.'

'Yes.'

'And then,' Sharmeen said slowly, 'he collapsed.'

'Yes.'

Aliya recalled her terror that night; she had screamed into the phone, calling out Amir's name. She had held the receiver and stared into the darkness of the room, sucked into a dark vortex, the world spinning violently around her.

'And then the doctor came...' prompted Sharmeen.

'Doctor Nawaz said that there was some internal bleeding and Amir should not have played the hero, he should have waited for medical help. His movements caused a haemorrhage in his brain and he collapsed on the road.'

Aliya grew silent once more. Sharmeen wanted to comfort her, but had discovered that when adults get lost in a distant space where they imagine the past and wish it were different, all you can do is wait for them to snap out of it.

'I'm just coming!' she said, springing up and throwing the comforter off her legs.

'Where are you going? It's a school night.'

'I know, I know. I just have to say goodnight to Abba.'

Sharmeen scampered into the hall and knocked lightly on the door opposite Aliya's room. She tip-toed to where her father lay on a hospital bed, slightly raised to an angle. Its metal rails were pulled down, there was no danger of him rolling over in his sleep. He was thin, shrivelled and frail. The hum and whir of the oxygen being pumped into him reassured Sharmeen. He was still breathing. The light outside the window cast an eerie blue halo on his gaunt face. There was something ghastly and unnatural in the way the oxygen tube invaded his nostrils. His lips seemed to have collapsed in exhaustion upon themselves. He looked like he was locked in perpetual anticipation—never peaceful, always waiting. His sallow skin was rough—Aziz had not shaved him today. She touched his cheek: his bristles were rebelliously sharp against her soft fingers. He was still around, with some help, although this sleeping individual with ashen skin and closed eyes was a far cry from the handsome man who had taught her how to play cards and taken long walks with her after coming home from office. Sharmeen planted a gentle kiss on his bald head—Aziz had shaved off his hair because it was falling off in clumps. An intricate grid of pale green and purple veins criss-crossed their way under his temples, as if trying to run away from the brown spots on his skin.

Doctor Nawaz had said that if he didn't come out of the coma soon, the chances of him ever regaining consciousness were slim. Her father had lain like this for close to six months now. Amma had begun to talk about this often, wondering if Abba would ever wake up. But what did she know? No, a coma was like a comma, a brief little pause, the sentence would still continue. There was always hope. Samarkand had hung on for years to be with his child. Her father wouldn't give up because he had to be there for her. He knew that she needed him.

'Wake up soon, Abba! I'm waiting for you!' she whispered in his ear before returning to her mother's bed, allowing herself to be pulled into a tight embrace. That night, she dreamt of Janeerees coming out of trucks and throwing webs at her father, while a falcon flapped towards them in the distance.

Chapter 3

'Let there be light!'

With one flick of the finger, Aziz hit the switch, flooding the room with a warm golden haze in stark contrast to the dark indigo of the night outside.

Sharmeen suspiciously surveyed the room for any untoward movements or shadows that would betray malevolent creatures lurking where they didn't belong. Dolls sat in the corner shelf: a frazzled looking Barbie with singed hair and a scarlet-topped Swedish piece with porcelain skin and wobbly green eyes. A teddy bear sat patiently between them, trying to maintain some semblance of masculine dignity, a serious and thoughtful look on his woolly face. She had given most of her toys away, but these three had remained. They had been gifts from her father.

'Aziz Bhai, I can't sleep here tonight.'

'Why not?'

'Because there are *creatures* in here. Can't you see?'

'You mean those lonely toy-friends of yours? They cry

to me and complain that it's been years since Sharmeen Bibi played with them.'

Sharmeen didn't tell Aziz that she'd had nightmares in which the Barbie had inched towards her with a malicious plastic grin while the teddy had laughed maniacally in the background, his eyes flashing red. Nani had told her that old abandoned toys were inhabited by Jinn to evoke panic in unsuspecting boys and girls. It seemed just the sort of dastardly thing that they would do. But that nightmare wasn't the real reason she hated this room.

'I'm too, too old to play with toys.'

'Who told you that?'

'No one, I decided myself.'

'Oh, so you're a grown-up, are you?'

'Yes.'

'But grown-ups aren't afraid of the dark,' Aziz challenged.

Sharmeen paused and stared at Aziz's white, starched kameez. He'd been around for as long as she could remember—serving, offering help, efficiently running the house and now, playing the role of attendant to her father. There was never a lie of hers he didn't see through.

'It's actually because of that huge tree next to the window,' she finally confessed. 'It's so...twisted. It doesn't allow the light through. It's...as if it wants to come inside. It taps my window at night. I don't like it. I don't want to let it in.'

'Bibi, it is just a tree.'

'Aziz Bhai, not everything is as it seems.'

'A tree is just a tree.'

'And that's why you are an ignorant scoundrel!'

Aziz whirled around to see Nani scowling at the door, her five-foot frame trembling with rage. Aziz stiffened in her presence, turning his gaze away from her grey eyes, promptly removing his hand from Sharmeen's shoulder.

'Tell me,' said Nani, walking inside and leaning heavily on her cane, 'don't you have anything better to do than stand around gaping in a young girl's room?'

'Aliya Bibi asked me to help Sharmeen Bibi get over her fear. She refuses to sleep in here.'

'Where a young girl sleeps is none of your business. Go prepare dinner. And clear up those chalk markings on the pavement. They look untidy.'

'But Nani, that's for my hopscotch!' protested Sharmeen.

Nani said nothing and continued to glare at Aziz's retreating form. He was tall and lithe, but his shoulders slouched in permanent submission to avoid untoward offence; a strategy that seldom worked as he still received sharp admonishment from Nani. After he left, she directed her scowl at her granddaughter, who felt increasingly uncomfortable with what had just transpired.

'You shouldn't talk to Aziz like that, Nani. He's my friend.'

'He's a man and you are about to be a young woman. You need to be careful of how close you get to him.'

Sharmeen didn't quite get what Nani meant, but let it go. She had understood well which battles she could and could not fight. When it came to Aziz, Nani would hear no sense. She bullied him like he was a despicable slave. Nana had taken Aziz off the streets and trained him to cook, clean and also to read and write. Aziz would have died for Sharmeen's grandfather, but the latter preceded him, extracting a promise to look after his wife and daughter. When Aliya married Amir, Aziz had accompanied them as major-domo, but he'd moved back in to Nani's house after the accident. Nani, who had rejoiced at his departure, now loathed him even more.

'Why were the two of you in this room, Sharmeen?'

'Amma sent me here with Aziz. She wanted me to do my homework here and I said I didn't want to because I wanted to stay in the living room.'

Nani scowled. 'She should have come with you herself. That girl is depending far too much on that mongrel.'

Sharmeen changed the subject before her grandmother launched into yet another attack on Aziz's character. 'Nani, don't you think there's something strange here? I can feel it. I try not to be scared, but I am.' She knew her grandmother understood. She always said fear was the sign of a logical and intelligent mind.

Nani walked in slowly, her cane tapping rhythmically against the mosaic floor. She stopped at the window, gazing at the tree outside. Her white hair shone in contrast against the mangled branches outside. Sharmeen fancifully thought that she looked like a white witch facing a dark foe.

'Do you know how a banyan grows, my love?' Nani asked, staring into the dark evening.

'No.'

'It's a parasite. A cancer,' Nani spat out, in a tone so

vicious that Sharmeen jumped. 'A few innocent seeds strewn by the winds of fate, land on a beautiful gulmohar tree, famed for its fiery flowers. Slowly, they find a nook, search out a crack: something to hold on to. They settle in and practice their dark magic. From them emerge the smallest of roots, selfish and strong. They creep and curl around, grasping, holding, growing. And they feed off the gulmohar, taking in its energy, their tendrils strangling it with their embrace. Soon, the roots become thick, pulsating branches that starve and trap their host within, eventually fisting deep into the ground. The gaunt gulmohar is allowed to survive, just barely, for it is the foundation that gave life to the banyan. If it dies, so does the banyan. And so it is that this tree outside the window thrives upon the carcass of the gulmohar. It *is* evil, my love. You are right to fear it.'

Nani's words did not reassure Sharmeen. She sidled up and put an arm around her grandmother's waist. 'At night, I see its shadows on my wall and they look like men trying to push against each other, struggling to enter my bedroom. But Amma says that the wood around the panes expands and contracts because of decreasing temperatures at night, and that's why I hear the creaks and groans.'

'Things that grow where they are not supposed to always want to invade what is good and pure, my love. We must take steps to protect you. Come.'

Nani marched off like a soldier on a mission, leaving Sharmeen to follow her into her bedroom. She took out a tarnished box from the cupboard and opened it. Inside lay a string of silver prayer beads, lazily recumbent and sinuous on a midnight blue velvet lining. Reverently Nani handed it to Sharmeen, who had made herself comfortable on the rocking chair.

'This belonged to my mother and my mother's mother before her. It's a special tasbeeh, you must be very careful with it. I want you to say a prayer on it, and repeat it one hundred times for seven days without fail. Promise me that you will?'

Sharmeen nodded, beginning to get even more nervous. Nani whispered something in her ear. It was one of the names of God: Ya-Khaliq.

'What does it mean, Nani?'

'It means "The Creator". Say it softly, under your breath. Quickly.'

'But why?'

'When you say His name, you summon protection from the other realm. This prayer arranges a strong force of defence.'

'*What* force of defence?' cried Sharmeen.

'Just trust me, my love. Say it now, while I watch over you. Good girl.'

Uncomfortable but eager to please, Sharmeen sat back down. Old people were scary: sometimes soft and sweet, sometimes mad and intense like Nani was now. Sharmeen looked at her grandmother's wide eyes, wrinkled skin and the large blue mole on her cheek. It would be better to oblige her than hurt her feelings by refusing. So Sharmeen closed her eyes and whispered the name.

Soft and steady, the consonants became familiar; after

the twentieth repetition her tongue moved of its own volition. A strange feeling of warmth, like a slow descending spiral, was pouring itself into her body. The sensation was pleasant. A red speck swirled around in the darkness underneath her lids. It grew and circled into neat little arabesques—flamboyant curves—twirling into a thousand different shapes, before plunging into itself again and again to form a beautiful yellow light.

Alarmed, Sharmeen opened her eyes. Her heart pounded as she looked at her grandmother, who smiled back, proudly.

***

When one is forced to sleep alone in a dark room and breathing becomes a chore, it is essential to take precautionary measures against imminent and pervasive danger. These involve: a thick blanket to keep unwanted elements out of one's immediate space; a torch to light up the darkness; and a book to distract the mind from every magnified sound that seems to portend doom.

Thus lay Sharmeen, trying to ignore the tap-tapping of the banyan on the window. Under the circumstances, she realized that the book she'd borrowed from the school library two days ago was probably not the best choice for night-time perusal. She'd stumbled upon it as she was browsing: an old hand-bound copy with a blue cloth-cover and tarnished copper binding. Coated in dust and shoved to the corner of the shelf by the new hardbound books, it had seemed to sulk like a little orphan pushed aside by its contemporary glossy peers. Its title was engraved: *The*

Historie of the Jinnaye and Other Invisible Folk. What such a book was doing in a middle-school library, she had no idea. But there it lay, hidden and enigmatic. Her father would have loved it. He thought old books, or 'vintage pieces' as he called them, were grand old things, holding not just stories but also imprints of the people who'd owned them through the ages. He cherished their yellowed pages and folded corners, their faint, greasy fingerprints, and the old, musty smell that had been lent to them by time.

Sharmeen opened the book and smelled the pages—they too smelled of old paper and a hint of vanilla. Under the bright torch-light she noticed the meticulously crafted illustrations with little notes on the side. She squinted at the faded print.

She snuggled deeper, spooked, but glad for books that offered a refuge from the chaos in her life. She usually sat in a little corner behind the bookshelves in the library at school, avoiding her classmates, most of whom she didn't much care for. It wasn't that she was unfriendly by nature—she was a new girl at this school, and Chambeli, a prissy little snot, teacher's pet and class monitor, had spread a rumour that Sharmeen had lice in her hair. Naturally, everyone avoided her. Besides, she really didn't have time for peer politics. Things like which boy-band was popular and which teacher had the biggest bum seemed frivolous compared to real concerns such as accidents, comas and invisible creatures.

She flipped through the pages and studied the drawings: there were Jinn with dog heads and dragon tails, and some looked like the figures drawn in Egyptian murals in her history book. There were tall figures that stretched up on the page, slim as her finger, with falcon and jackal heads and horned heads and feathered faces.

She read that the greatest civilizations on earth had been constructed by Jinn who had repented their rebellion against God, or those who had been chained by His command. She read descriptions of a massive city under the sea for water-demons, called Naai'dda, the strongest and most powerful of Jinn. Sharmeen wondered if the Naai'dda were the same things as Naiads that she'd read about in books on Greek mythology with her father when he had been well. How she wished she could show him this book! She missed their bedtime discussions intensely. She wondered if Abba would agree with her theory that the great city under the sea was the lost world of Atlantis. Perhaps it wasn't so lost? Perhaps the Jinn had made it appear so because they wanted their privacy?

According to the book, the Jinn were incredibly private folk who preferred to keep to themselves and were quite territorial, fighting with each other for private spaces that could not be disturbed by Man. Sharmeen's eyes skimmed the pages, sleep glazing her eyes, and she wondered idly how the Jinn felt about the population explosion that had taken place in most parts of the world. They loved lagoons and forests and ancient burial sites—and these were slowly being encroached upon by human civilization. She was sure her father would agree with the newly formed theory buzzing in her brain: if Jinn controlled the elements, then perhaps the tsunamis, earthquakes and tornados were all just really irate creatures punishing mankind for multiplying?

Sharmeen shut the book and slipped it under the bed. Lying back, she covered her face with the blanket, her wonder numbed by the more powerful urge to sleep. She could still hear the tapping of the banyan, and now more than ever she imagined that it wasn't just the tree, but some invisible spirit knocking at her window, wanting her to open it so that it could come inside. Fortunately, the thought of Nani sleeping in the room across comforted her; as did her assurance that the prayers of the past seven days had laid a mantle of divine protection upon her. Whether this was true or not, she didn't know, but slowly she drifted off into a sleep unplagued by nightmares.

Chapter 4

For those who watch and know where to look, omens are everywhere. Two mynahs portend love, a solitary one signals bereavement. An anthill in the grass means prosperity; its destruction heralds poverty. These ancient wisdoms were too often dismissed as mere superstitions, but Nani had no concern with what people thought. She was the Watcher, destined to be thus by her lineage, and she observed everything. Patrolling the estate at a steady amble, her sharp eyes missed nothing. Every flower, blade of grass, every living creature had sanctuary here. Nothing could be killed—not geckos, not cockroaches, not ants, not worms. The garden had bloomed into a small forest with long grass and thick-leaved trees.

Danger was creeping slowly towards the house—the signs were manifesting themselves. Yesterday a beheaded cat had been discovered outside the gate. The water in the fountain behind the old well had turned a tepid yellow a week before that. And now Sharmeen had sensed the evil of the banyan, which contained in it a terrible secret of usurpation and murder. These were no mere coincidences. In the early light of dawn, Nani stood on the pavement where her granddaughter played hopscotch. With her cane she etched invisible figures on the chalked squares, muttering prayers of protection to ward off evil. Using her cane like a pen in the air, she wrote several names of God, carefully, strategically drawing their energies to wall in, protect, and to keep out that which had the freedom of mischief. A final flourish and a prayer sealed off the charm. The dry leaves of the banyan in the wind sounded like paper being crushed in an angry fist. She stood up and massaged her spine, consumed by the presence of the dark energy that was steadily increasing its power. She was familiar with it; it made her listless but she was too wise to succumb to it, recognizing it as a prelude to despair—the territory of evil spirits. As long as she had breath in her body, she would protect her family. The darkness would not win, not on her watch. Nani faced the house and sensed the gaze at last. She narrowed her eyes and stood defiant. 'I am ready,' she said.

***

Sharmeen held a smooth pebble and prepared to throw it carefully into the designated square. It wasn't a question of aim but force—too gentle a toss and she'd miss, too hard and she'd overthrow. Concentration was key. It was Girl and Stone against Chalk and Number.

This was her favourite part of the day—post-school and

pre-homework, playing hopscotch in the late afternoon. Today had been a whopping nightmare at school. The librarian had yelled at all the students for making too much noise and a general eviction had ensued, wherein she too was included, even though she'd been reading quietly in her corner.

Then her Math teacher had called her dumb because she couldn't understand the probability sums, and the whole class had laughed and Chambeli had primly raised her hand and given the correct answer. Sharmeen had wanted to slap the complacent smile off her pasty little face.

Her concentration was broken by Aziz who called out from the kitchen: 'Sharmeen Bibi, your mother is calling you inside.'

'What for?' Sharmeen yelled in between squares, tottering on one leg like a drunk flamingo.

'You need to drink your milk. You didn't have any for breakfast.'

'But I haven't finished my game!'

'Aliya Bibi says...'

'I'll be there in a while, Aziz Bhai!' interrupted Sharmeen, grumbling to herself. Milk. Vile substance forced on generations of children to make them grow up faster so that they could become worried and boring adults who took years of milk-drinking frustration out on hapless little children who were too busy playing and getting on with things.

She picked up another pebble. Pursing her lips, she sliced the small stone through the air, watching it settle on the last square. Practice had made her perfect and in a few jumps, she'd be home. Tucking wayward strands of hair behind her ear, Sharmeen closed her fingers in tight fists and began to jump. One skip, two and three. Just as she was about to make the final leap, Aziz's voice interrupted her concentration.

'Sharmeen Bibi, Aliya Bibi is very angry you haven't come inside yet.'

Instinctively, Sharmeen turned around to the sound of his voice, just as she jumped the last square. And the world went still—the way it tends to do when one realizes a painful fall is imminent. Sharmeen inhaled sharply, bracing herself for the rude shock of impact that was sure to come. The banyan tree tilted in her line of vision. This was going to be bad. Closing her eyes, she waited for the pain.

But, like the twist in Nani's tales, something odd happened as she fell. Her head was a fraction away from the pavement when she felt a gentle lift, a force gliding her over the squares and laying her on the cement. She felt as light as a feather swaying in the breeze. It was most disconcerting, like running down stairs and expecting an extra step that isn't there.

Sharmeen exhaled. Slowly, she rose and stood up, brushing the dirt off her jeans. She was about a foot away from the hopscotch squares on the ground.

She was unharmed, unscratched and unsettled. What had just happened? Perhaps the sun was very hot and it had affected her brain, as her mother was always predicting it would.

She walked towards the house, putting her hands in her pockets to stop them from shaking. At the door, Aziz had observed all that had occurred, his expression unreadable.

***

Sharmeen walked down the long, narrow corridor that led to the living room. Spooked by her 'fall', she hardly noticed the black-and-white portrait of her great-great-great grandfather who stared glumly at all passers-by, harbouring a look of unrelieved constipation. Nor did she register his mother, a handsome woman whose bold gaze scanned the entire corridor.

What she did notice, however, was that all the female relatives had been depicted in their youth, and yet, their hair was snowy white, like Nani's. Sharmeen figured that maybe this was a genetic quirk that had skipped a generation because her mum's hair was still brown. She fervently hoped to be spared as well—she didn't want to look old before her time.

Nani's house had been built well before World War II. Its roof sloped downwards, held together with wooden beams that formed a grid around the slabs of cement in between them. Long, tapering cracks snaked along the slabs, as if they were tired of holding the roof up for more than half a century.

It was a building meant to be explored, and when she had first moved in here, she had done just that. Keyholes and crevices beckoned, hinges creaked when doors were left closed for far too long. The woodwork seemed to sag in the humidity. Decay had set in with time; paint had peeled and marble had cracked. Rumour had it that the house had once hosted prisoners of war and that their souls still haunted the empty spaces of the unused second storey. Nani said they were not ghosts, but Jinn who had fallen in love with the building and adopted it.

'Young lady, Aziz and I have been calling and calling! When I say it's time to come inside, it's time to come inside. What took you so long?' demanded Aliya, as her daughter finally walked into the living room. She was curled up on Nana's chair, wearing an old shalwar kameez that had softened with time and frequent washing. Sharmeen noticed that Aliya no longer bothered about her appearance; no make-up, no freshly ironed clothes, no meticulously wrapped chignon into which her father would slide a flower. No, there was just an impatient and untidy ponytail.

'I was playing my game.'

'Don't answer back.'

Feigning a bored defiance, Sharmeen flopped down against the coffee table, eyeing the glass of milk suspiciously.

'Hurry up and drink it. Don't make me scold you further.'

Scrunching up her face, she gulped, grimacing as the thick liquid made a viscous trail down her throat.

'This is awful.'

'Arey Bibi,' said Aziz, walking in with a plate of French fries, 'milk is the drink of the heavens! Rivers of it have been promised to those who listen to their parents and God.'

'*I* don't want to go to heaven if all I get to drink is milk!' she remarked, reaching greedily for her favourite snack. 'Thank you, Aziz Bhai!'

Aziz chuckled with pleasure. 'So would you prefer hell, then?'

'Nani says hell is where all the interesting people end up.' Aliya frowned. 'I wish you wouldn't quote her all the time. Or take her so seriously. She is old and...dotty.'

Aziz chuckled, but stopped immediately as the subject of the conversation walked in. He sighed in resignation at her expression of displeasure. He'd been held in contempt so many times that nervousness was now giving way to weariness. But this time, Nani's ire wasn't directed exclusively at him: it also included her daughter. Aliya looked guilty, and hid her face behind a fashion magazine that she'd suddenly become interested in.

'Dotty, did you say? Indeed I must be so. Only a dotty woman can house her daughter and comatose son-in-law, tolerate this simpering parasite that skulks along beside them and *still* be subjected to their ridicule. I'm not dotty, I'm mad. Why don't you just go ahead and say it?'

Aliya looked contrite for a moment. 'Amma, I shouldn't have said what I did...but believe me, I wouldn't be here if I didn't have to. It's no walk in the park for me either.'

'But you meant it, didn't you?'

'I don't have the energy to argue with you right now.'

'Aliya Bibi has a headache, Begum Sahib,' Aziz interjected.

'You shut up! Do not presume to intrude upon matters

of family! Know your place...go snoop around somewhere out of my sight!'

'Amma, don't talk to him like that!' snapped Aliya.

'And how do *you* talk about me? In front of that scoundrel and my granddaughter. I am your mother!'

'And you scare *my* daughter with your stories and superstitions.'

'They are *not* superstitions!'

'I don't want to listen to anything more you have to say.' Aliya flung the magazine on the coffee table and stood up to face her mother. 'Why can you not respect the fact that I don't want you telling my daughter the stories that you brought *me* up with?'

'They are not stories!'

'Yes, they are. Do you have any idea what effect your nonsense has on a young child's imagination? If you want to live in your world of horror and doom, so be it. But leave the rest of us to try and come to grips with reality.'

'It is because of my so-called "superstitions" that this family is intact!'

'Intact? We fight all the time, mainly because you will not respect anyone else's desire for sanity. It's always been you, your way and your ridiculous fantasies!'

'*Ridiculous* you call them!' roared Nani, thumping her cane on the ground.

'I do! Ever since I was a little girl, I was scared of my own shadow because you told me it might come alive and eat me. "Aliya, don't wave that spoon—a demon will haunt you." "Aliya, don't cut your nails, they invite poltergeists!"

"Don't comb your hair at night; some Jinn will possess you." Sparrows signal chaos, black crows will bring death. Well guess what, Amma, we're *surrounded* by black crows. Look outside! I don't see anyone popping off! I threw salt over my shoulders, looked out for cracks and did all kinds of stupid things because *you* made me. I used to have nightmares and Abba used to hold me at night to comfort me. I will not let you do the same thing to Sharmeen!'

The young person in question, again finding herself in the midst of a battle, finished her milk quickly, hoping her offering would affect some sort of truce.

Nani raised her chin, both haughty and incensed. 'Your father never understood that it was *I* who took care of this family. *I* have lived in this house all my life. *I* have a responsibility to protect it; I have seen my mother and my mother's mother use the same mumbo-jumbo that you scoff at. And I tried to teach you, but you ran away because you are a coward! Always have been. All you do is sit around this rodent your father dragged in, scold your daughter and blame *me* for what happened to Amir. Face life. Start to live on your own feet, rather than lean on *my* doddering ones and curse *me* for my strength.'

Aliya rubbed her temples. 'Amma,' she said in a hoarse whisper, 'my husband is in a coma in the next room, fighting for his life. There is *nothing* I can do about it. It makes me angry to be so helpless, but helpless I am because *these things happen.* There is *no one* I can fight with. I have struggled with this and it's *not* helping that you think he can be saved by reading a few mantras and waving magic sticks in the air. The doctor has said it's a matter of time. Do you have any idea how much agony it is to wait and watch him slip away?'

Sharmeen scrambled up and hugged her mother, whose shining eyes and trembling shoulders showed just how broken she was feeling. But Nani was unaffected.

'I have a quitter for a daughter. I'm disappointed in you.'

Aliya suppressed a sob.

Sharmeen was horrified. 'Amma, don't cry. Nani didn't mean it. Please.'

Aliya stroked Sharmeen's hair. 'I think I'll go lie down for a bit, my love. I need a break.'

Sharmeen stared after her mother; feeling helpless, not knowing how to comfort the hurt her grandmother had caused.

'Nani, *why* are you so mean to her?'

But Nani was unrepentant. 'It is the habit of the weak to whimper at every calamity. That is all.' She walked out of the room, leaving Sharmeen frustrated. She wanted to hate her grandmother—the alarming frequency with which Nani made her mum cry would have turned any child against her. Yet, there was an undercurrent of truth to what she had said. Her mother *had* given up after Abba's accident—reliving the past again and again. In some ways, Nani articulated what Sharmeen could not for fear of hurting her mother's feelings—but sometimes, just sometimes, it would be nice to see her mother hopeful, optimistic, if only to reassure her.

This was why she needed Nani. She was old enough to

understand how her obsession with the unseen could be overwhelming for a person as rational as her mum. But the 'facts' that her mother kept talking about had made her give up too easily, killed her hopes too soon with too deft a stroke. Predictions of death, statistics of survival would make anyone despair. Nani's stories were alarming, but they gave her hope. There was always something that could be *done,* a twist to be hoped for. This was what her mother didn't understand. In a family where all the adults were trapped in their own little worlds, Nani's stories gave her comfort.

Aziz, who had retreated into the kitchen, now came towards her.

'Where is Aliya Bibi?'

'Gone to her room.'

'That is good. She needs her rest. These fights exhaust her so,' he said, his voice laced with concern. 'And Sharmeen must finish her homework quickly so that her mother will be happy with her?'

Sharmeen nodded and dragged herself to her room. This afternoon, with the milk and the fight, had sunk into unpleasantness. She ran quickly to her father's side and planted a kiss on his forehead. Fortified by the assurance that he was still here and still breathed, she left to complete her homework.

Chapter 5

When your left eye twitched, bad luck was on its way, which didn't bode well for Sharmeen. Pressing on the eyelid with a firm finger didn't make it stop. She tossed and turned, trying to ignore the rat-a-tat-tat of the scratching banyan and the *bin-binnining* of an annoying mosquito by her ear. The night was hot and she was irritable, so she flung off her blanket, grabbed her pillow and ran off to Nani's bed and lay down beside her.

But sleep did not come, partly because Nani was snoring, partly because Sharmeen hadn't forgotten her almost-fall in the afternoon. She wanted to talk about it, but didn't want to wake Nani up. Trying to imitate her grandmother, she scowled so as to intimidate any dark energy that happened to be lingering in the atmosphere. Time passed and nothing happened. Boredom beckoned sleep. Her eyes fluttered shut just as a blanket was drawn over her legs. She turned and saw that Nani was still fast asleep.

But then who had moved the blanket?

Her heart started pounding. Awake and terrified once again, she scooted closer to Nani, wide eyes scanning for any suspicious activity. But there was the gentle sway of the curtains and the whirring of the ceiling fan. All was still. She lay silently for a few moments, until fear finally overcame consideration, and she poked her sleeping grandmother firmly in the back.

Nani stirred and turned around, her eyes slowly registering the presence of a small, trembling body next to her.

'Sharmeen? What are you doing here, my love?'

'Nothing.'

'Then why are you trembling?'

'I'm...n-not.'

'N-no? N-not afraid?'

'Nani! Don't make fun of me.'

'What has you scared?'

'I'm not scared, okay? But something odd is happening. I know it.' She told her about her fall-turned-into-flight in the early afternoon. 'And then just now, someone put the blanket over my legs and it wasn't you. I can feel someone watching me. Am I going mad?'

Nani smiled. 'So it has begun.'

Sharmeen's heart banged against her ribs. '*What* has begun?'

Her grandmother sat up against the headboard, suddenly deep in thought. This was not a good sign. Nani never weighed her words with Sharmeen, believing in the policy of uncensored truth at all times. But now she chose her words carefully.

'It is time that I told you about my great-great-great grandmother. You must be ready for what you hear. Forces beyond my control are nosing their way here and you need to be armed with knowledge and protected by what you have summoned.'

'WHAT have I summoned?'

'The women of this house have always been helped by the Jinn in their time of need. Whenever we have called, they have answered. For seven days you summoned yours, and now he is here.'

Sharmeen blinked and her mouth fell open. 'I'm not sure I want him to stick around.'

'Hush. You do not invite a guest to your home and then ask him to leave. Besides, you need not fear him.'

'Um, let's talk about something else,' said Sharmeen, growing increasingly uncomfortable by how her grandmother's stories had suddenly invaded real life. Her mother's warnings about Nani's sanity rang in her ear.

'Yes, let's talk about my great-great-great grandmother, because it all started with her. Her name was Nayntara, which means a twinkle in the eye. She was just like a small star in the early dawn sky: bright, mischievous with a tinkling laugh, her face haloed by long, silken hair, black as the night sky. Many men wanted to marry her, but were intimidated by her intelligence. She had a gaze that seemed to pierce into their very souls, reading their thoughts, which weren't terribly interesting in the first place. So they kept their distance. Her father despaired at her unconventional ways—her midnight walks and her preference for solitude over society and parties, and all the pretty things that young women were supposed to fancy.'

To Sharmeen, she didn't sound different from Nani, though Nani was not beautiful. No, her features reminded one of a cliff next to a raging ocean, hard and ridged; not pretty, but majestic. 'So she too had a Jinn?'

'No, she had an imagination, which is what most attracts Jinn to humans. Her father was concerned that she was too peculiar to ever find a husband, so he forced her to marry a man his own age—Khanjee: a gambler renowned for his recklessness and roving eye. Nayntara was distraught, and to add to her woes her father died soon after the wedding. She moved in with her husband to this house once more, for back then it was a grand estate with much prestige. Besides, Khanjee needed to sell his own home to get out of debt.

'From the beginning, Khanjee tried to subdue the young Nayntara. The wedding night was difficult and his attentions were cruel. The henna had not completely dried on her hands when she became a woman. As her husband snored beside her, she slipped out into the garden and sat down under a gulmohar. The sound of her soft crying, the tinkle of her anklets and the warm moistness of her henna awoke a Jinn who lived in the tree.'

'How come all the Jinn in your stories live in trees, Nani?' asked Sharmeen.

'Oh, because Jinn love gardens, you know, and they have a particular attachment to trees. You can tell a lot about a Jinn from the home it chooses. A spirit of a weeping willow is morose and sadistic, like our Janeeree. A Jinn in a banyan will never be up to any good—for it has chosen a tree that will never flower. That of a gulmohar is beautiful—inside and out—living for beauty and fragrance rather than malice. Such a one was this creature, who sniffed Nayntara's feet, crept up her calves and entered her body through her hair, falling in love with her instantly. He told her to not be scared and promised to always look after her. He carried her away...soaring high into the sky, above the white clouds bathed in pale moonlight. Do you know how to spot a Jinn travelling in the sky, Sharmeen?'

Sharmeen shook her head.

'Well, sometimes Jinn float in the air on little rafts made of vapour. You really should study the clouds, for they hold many secrets. Sometimes you see feathery wisps just beneath the sky, moving separately, as if detached. Those are the ones used by the Jinn: soft, misty mattresses to snooze on, letting the wind pull them in any direction. Such a cloud was used by the Jinn of the garden to show Nayntara the stars. She fell in love with this new world he showed her, full of magic and promise. During the day, her old, wrinkled husband's love bruised, wounded and invaded her, but at night the passion of the Jinn offered her liberation. She found that she had strength to withstand a miserable marriage with a powerful ally by her side. Nothing Khanjee said or did hurt her now, for she knew that at night, she would soar high with her Jinn.

'But all jealous husbands instantly know when their wives have a secret. Nayntara's distracted smiles bothered

Khanjee. He increased his attentions and when she remained distant, the beatings began and only stopped when she was pregnant with his child.'

'How could the Jinn allow all this?'

'Oh he didn't want to, but he was one of the pure beings. We think of Jinn as monsters, but like men, they are agents of free will. They too have been sent down from heaven with a choice to do either good or evil. This Jinn had sworn a sacred oath to God never to hurt a human being; if he broke it, he would be barred from heaven forever. So he watched his beloved's anguish. He lay with her when her husband left the bed, stroking her hair and caressing her belly, beneath which her daughter grew. Those were sweet moments, until Nayntara dreamed of a giant crow flying towards her, flapping its ugly wings, their reverberation tearing at her eardrums. She awoke and told the Jinn, and he knew it was a sign of her death. She implored him to take care of her daughter after she had gone. And as much as he would have loved to float away with the soul of his beloved into the land where all is forgotten, he promised to stay back and look after her daughter.'

'That's so sad,' sniffed Sharmeen.

'She died two nights after her daughter Anisa was born. As Anisa grew up, she too began to escape into the garden to flee her oppressive father. And slowly, the Jinn made himself known to her. She was scared at first, but he gained her trust by telling her stories of her mother. And she grew fond of him and began to prefer his company above anyone else's. Again, Khanjee became suspicious. He locked her in her room and informed her that she was to marry one of his debtors and move to another city.

'The Jinn could not see the suffering of his beloved's child, who was like his own. So he flew to the wise son of Samarkand and appealed to him for help, as many Jinn often did, for he was a bridge between them and humans. Traverser of Both Worlds, he could draw on all sorts of earthly and supernatural energies. He gave the Jinn the same string of silver beads that Samarkand had gifted to the Janeeree, on which the Amluq had bestowed the power to summon Jinn when the bearer of the beads was in need. He stipulated a Divine Name that was to be read for seven days and seven nights.'

Sharmeen's eyes widened. 'Did she read what I read?'

'Yes, my love, she did. On the same beads—they are a family heirloom and our greatest secret. On the eighth day, another Jinn was summoned to serve her. Except that this one was young and powerful and had sworn no oath to prevent him from doing harm.'

'Wasn't he dangerous? Couldn't he have hurt Anisa as well?'

'He certainly could have, but didn't, because he chose not to. Good and evil are not characteristics, my love; they are choices and this new Jinn had learnt, after much mischief, to control his dark side. Which didn't mean that he couldn't unleash it whenever he wished, and unleash it he did, but only on Khanjee, haunting his dreams, shaking the bed violently so that even consciousness did not release him from the nightmares he sought refuge from. When

Khanjee tried to hit Anisa, the Jinn flung him across the room so hard that he cracked a rib. Khanjee accused his daughter of black magic, but she ignored him. Anisa told him firmly that she would *never* marry his debtor, or be hit again.'

'Did Khanjee believe her?'

'Oh yes, he did. He watched her warily and did not dare to impose his will on her in any way. After he died, she married a man of her own choice; and when her husband offered her protection, she released her Jinn from any obligation towards her.'

'But what happened to the first Jinn, Nani?'

'He had fulfilled his promise to his beloved. Now his ward was under the protection of a stronger entity. So he floated up to heaven, where a tiny woman with twinkling eyes awaited him with open arms. And before Anisa died, she passed her secret to her daughter, who passed it on to me. This is a gift given to us, my love, for we are the friends of the Jinn and can communicate with them and summon them in our times of need.'

Sharmeen thought about all the portraits in the hall. 'Nani, how come all of my grandmothers have such brilliant white hair?'

Nani smiled. 'White hair is the mark of the Watcher—of the women and men who look out for invisible beings, read their symbols and sense their arrival. The Jinn are selective creatures and will not lift the curtain on their world to just any old body, you know. They converse with few, and associate with even fewer, revealing themselves only when they must.'

'You have white hair.'

'Yes.'

'So you also have a Jinn with you?'

'Always have.'

Sharmeen's mind reeled with what Nani had just told her. She began to recall strange little instances that she had dismissed without further thought. Instances such as her grandmother knowing where to look when things disappeared and finding them in impossible places—like finding a ruby ring in the middle of a locked carton in the storeroom, or a wad of cash tucked away carefully in Abba's shoe at the back of the cupboard. She remembered the night Nani told her the story of Samarkand, and the slipper that had moved into her hand.

'Nani, did your Jinn pull the blanket over me just now?'

Nani looked away, as if conferring with an invisible creature. 'No, my love. That was probably yours.'

Sharmeen gulped hard. She thought it was too intimate a gesture for someone she had not yet made acquaintance with.

'Nani, I don't want a Jinn. How do I send him back?'

'You are ungrateful, child. He takes care of your comfort, prevents you from breaking your arm when you play hopscotch and you return his consideration by a desire to send him away?'

Sharmeen didn't know what to believe. 'Why can't I see him?'

'Because you are too afraid. Fear clouds the mind and vision, and you must look at what is rather than what you want to see. To witness the world of Jinn, you must have courage—for it is the world of the unknown, full of turmoil and trouble, but also beauty and love. One cannot be like your mother, ready to give up in the daylight. One has to be ready to traverse the darkness to be able to get a glimmer of their kind.'

Struck by a devastating thought, Sharmeen interrupted, 'Nani, will my hair turn white if I talk to him?'

Nani chuckled. 'Not immediately. But yes, slowly, you too will be from the line of Watchers. It is a great honour, my love, but also an immense responsibility.'

'Is my Jinn listening to me now?'

'How do I know? I only know about mine.'

'And what is your Jinn like?'

Nani turned and looked at the rocking chair. She snickered.

'He's a bit tired of pushing your slippers from under the bed.'

Sharmeen stiffened.

'Tell him I'm sorry.'

'He says he's used to it.'

'Nani, I'm not sure about any of this.'

'Of course, you aren't. Faith will come slowly, when fear has gone. Now come close and go to sleep. But before you do, remember this. You will only see your Jinn when you stop being afraid. And there is plenty to come that will test your courage, my love. You have to protect yourself and your mother as well. I sense an evil slowly taking root.'

'Do you mean the banyan, Nani?'

'Other forces as well. Some of which I do not understand myself. But that is why I gave the beads to you, my love. Not even your mother knows about them, and we must keep it that way. She will not believe any of this and think you've gone mad too. But your Jinn will protect you, if you let him.'

'Right now I've got you and your Jinn. I don't need to see anyone or anything else.'

Nani gave her a pat and cuddled her close. Sharmeen fell asleep in her grandmother's arms, while the latter gazed at shadows of the leaves dancing against the white screen of her window.

Chapter 6

Aziz stood in the afternoon heat of the kitchen—the hottest room in the house. Beads of sweat trickled down his back; a pedestal fan mounted on the wall opposite the stove was the only form of cooling to provide relief from the oppressive gloom of the summer.

He poured boiling water into the glass bowl. It bubbled as it touched the clump of sticky, brown tamarind seeds that lay in fearful anticipation of a hateful end. He took a metal spoon and grinded them. Swirls of red spiralled slowly, infusing the water with a murky hue. A maze of memories came alive in Aziz's mind: images of the past, vivid from frequent recollection. He was transported from the kitchen to a summer garden, playing with Aliya, as usual.

Pakran pakrai, oonch neech, teelo express. His favourite had been baraf paani: now he was frozen, now her touch made him gush forth to chase her, as she ran away from him, screaming in feigned terror. How happy their games had been in the speckled sunshine beneath the trees!

He had been her companion, helping her comb her dolls' golden hair, looking away obediently when she bathed them. He played house with her, and doctor-doctor and a hundred other games. He imagined them growing up like this, brother and sister, always laughing, always having an adventure, always together.

And then one day, he kissed her on the cheek. He was eight and she was ten. Aliya giggled, but Begum Sahib had seen.

Begum Sahib had bellowed with rage, grabbing him by his elbow and dragging him so mercilessly he had feared his arm would come out of its socket. She threw him into the store room and locked him there.

How terrified he'd been! He had trembled and cried and begged to be let out, but Begum Sahib had shown no pity. The chowkidar had brought a charpoy in the store, which was to serve as Aziz's bedroom, he was told. The next day, while Aliya was at school and Sahib at work, Begum Sahib had summoned Aziz to inform him of his new position in the house. He was to learn to serve them breakfast, lunch and dinner, after which he was to retire to his quarters and not mingle with them. They were his benefactors, they had provided him protection, but he was to remember that he was an outsider and must remain so. Aziz spent the next few frightening days chopping onions till his eyes burned, cutting red peppers and rubbing his face not knowing any better, so that his eyes burned with hot tears.

The worst punishment was his separation from Aliya,

who had been forbidden from visiting him in the kitchen. She tried to go behind her mother's back, but soon, school had brought with it its own priorities. She had other, more appropriate friends to spend her time with. The memory of their childhood days dimmed, and she came to terms with Aziz's new role, despite having vague misgivings that perhaps something more was owed to him.

Even Sahib had protested weakly and then returned to his books and rocking chair. Aziz bristled at the injustice of his situation. To have known the intimacy of family, of love and then to be rudely removed from it was a wound that festered through the decades. In his spare time, he read tales of hate, where men avenged the loss of lovers, and women unearthed the bodies of their mothers-in-law and gnawed on their livers.

Aziz returned to the present. He spooned some burnt-orange chilli powder and sprinkled it on the paste, making it more acrid. He sniffed as he stirred the khatti daal and tasted it. It was more bitter than sweet, but it would do.

***

Crows are clever creatures—they caw to each other, swoop and slide in air-play, use twigs and stones to beat their food and crack it open. They are tricksters and tyrants, edging the tiny mynas out to claim a territory for themselves. It is the code of the crow to watch out for its kind—to defend, forage and unite for the flock. So when one of them is butchered, they congregate in a murder, their black gazes watching for the assassin.

Two days had passed since Sharmeen found out about her Jinn, and nothing had changed, thankfully. She went to school, same as usual. Nothing untoward occurred, so Nani's alarming predictions were brushed aside in favour of school and homework. But this afternoon, as she got off the school bus and walked up the driveway, she saw the crows huddled together, black and sombre on the roof of the house and on the branches of the gulmohar and banyan; dark sentinels gazing with silent disapproval at a mutilated confederate. A pike stood in the centre of the numbered squares where she played hopscotch. On its sharp, diamond end was impaled a large crow, its black beak pointing to the sky, its body upturned, twisted and wrung with savage butchery.

Sharmeen stared at it, aghast, and then at the crows that had now surrounded her. Their cadaverous gazes seemed to accuse her of a heinous crime. She broke into a run just as they began to caw and flap their wings, as if preparing for an attack. Their raucous calls brought Aliya to the door.

'Come inside quickly, Sharmeen! They've been like this all morning.'

'Amma, what happened?'

Aliya bit her lip, wringing her hands, staring outside, then at Sharmeen and then back out, as if looking for an answer.

'It's your grandmother, Sharmeen.'

'What's happened to her?'

Aliya took Sharmeen's bag and ushered her down the corridor. 'She's a bit disoriented—she saw the dead crow on the pike and collapsed.'

'Why?'

'I think she's in shock. You know how she takes everything to be an omen.'

Sharmeen ran to her grandmother's room. It was dark, the curtains drawn. Nani lay in bed, staring at the ceiling with glazed eyes. Sharmeen climbed on to the covers, her Bata shoes still on, and looked at her face. Her lips were pale, cracked dry like broken clay.

'What's happened?' she asked.

At the sound of her voice, Nani turned. Some colour returned to her cheeks as she registered that her granddaughter's eyes were wide with confusion and concern.

'Sharmeen,' she croaked, 'you are here.'

'Yes. I'm here. I saw the crow.'

Nani searched Sharmeen's face, her eyes shining madly. 'Sharmeen, my moon, you must listen to me very carefully. It is an omen, my love. Do you remember the dream I told you about? The one my great-great-great grandmother had?'

'Of the crow with the flapping wings? Yes.'

'Evil has struck its first blow. I should have been prepared, but I didn't know it would come this soon. We are in grave danger.'

'Nani, stop this,' she begged, frustrated at this crossing over of night fantasies into the reality of the broad afternoon.

'I cannot. It is done. The pact has been violated.'

'The pact?'

'The pact our ancestors made with the Jinn to leave us in peace for as long as we didn't harm an innocent creature on these grounds. They let us have this land my love, and now we've broken their rules. I was waiting to for you to grow older to tell you all about it. So much to tell, so much to pass on...but no time.'

'Nani, nothing is going to happen to you. I won't allow it.'

'Something *is* coming. I can feel it in my bones. Did you see them outside? They bear witness to the act of murder. They raise their protest to the sky and Death hears. He is coming. The talisman has been broken.'

'What talisman? The kind you put in necklaces and things?'

'No, Sharmeen,' interrupted Nani impatiently, her eyes roving madly over her granddaughter's face, knobbly fingers clutching at her sleeve with frenzy born of haste. 'Talismans are charms, made of numbers that protect or destroy. I had made one of them on the ground where you play hopscotch, to protect you from anyone who wished you harm. Someone has entered and mutilated a creature of nature and you are unprotected now. All is out of sequence...an act of murder...to be avenged only by death.'

'Nani, please stop.'

'No, you must listen, even if it is not what you want to hear. Someone in this house wants to harm us.'

'Nani, you're hyperventilating.' Sharmeen held on to her grandmother's slender shoulders, which seemed all the more fragile in her state. But her grandmother was in no mood to be placated.

'Listen to me. You must seek out your Jinn. He is

the only one who can protect you now. Promise me you will.'

'Nani,' Sharmeen protested.

'*Promise?*'

'I promise.'

'Good.'

And with that, Nani lay her head back down and closed her eyes. Sharmeen held out her hand under her grandmother's nose to check for breath. The warm air on her fingers reassured her—she was just asleep.

Sharmeen walked out to see Aliya conferring with Aziz, both of whom stood outside Nani's room like naughty children, exiled in punishment.

'Is Begum Sahib all right?' asked Aziz.

'She refused to talk to me,' Aliya complained.

Sharmeen thought about telling them the truth, but decided against it, mostly because she knew her mum would just take all this as final confirmation that Nani had taken permanent leave of her senses. 'No, she just wanted to see if I was okay.'

Aliya sighed and rubbed her temples. It had been a long day.

'Aliya Bibi, do you have a headache?' Aziz asked, his sharp eyes missing nothing.

'A small one,' she confessed.

'Perhaps you need a little more rest. You've been up since dawn. Why don't you take a nap now? I can wake you up in an hour.'

'You shouldn't fuss over me, Aziz. We should call for

Doctor Nawaz, however. Just to make sure Amma is okay. Such anxiety attacks are not normal, even for her. I've been after her to get a check-up done, but she's so stubborn.'

Sharmeen didn't think that was a good idea. Nani thought that all doctors were idiots, trusting medicine over prayer. Moreover, she was an impossible patient— uncooperative, rude and generally obnoxious to anyone who dared prescribe medication for ailments best given time to run their course. The suffering of the body cleansed the soul, and it was through the soul that the body could be healed. She firmly believed this and used Amir as an example of the failed approach of modern medicine. She would not take kindly to Doctor Nawaz's visit—it would agitate her further. Aziz agreed, saying it was probably better to wait and see how Begum Sahib fared after her rest. 'In the meantime, I should go to Amir Sahib; it's time for his exercise. With all the commotion this morning, I haven't had a chance to check on him.'

'I'll help you,' piped in Sharmeen, who didn't need an excuse to be with her father.

She went with Aziz and saw him get to work. He was very methodical, folding the sheet, turning her father gently, lifting his hands, then his feet, massaging his fingers, pressing, pulling, rotating them deftly to keep the joints as supple as possible.

'How strong Abba's nails still are!' she remarked.

'Hair and nails have a will of their own. Did you know they continue to grow even after death, even though a corpse has begun to rot? Many a gravedigger has confirmed this to be true.'

'Gravedigger? Do you know one, Aziz Bhai?'

'Oh no, I don't, but if you read the newspapers, you'll know that some men dig the dead up and steal from them.'

'They do?'

'Yes. The fruit-seller told me the other day that graveyard thieves are becoming quite a menace. They dig up corpses in the cemetery behind the old vegetable bazaar. They take clothes, jewellery—bones, as well.'

'Aziz Bhai, don't tell me about such awful things,' protested Sharmeen, shivering. She'd had enough talk of death from her grandmother today and couldn't handle any more. Graveyards and vegetables—it almost made one think of rotting corpses providing fertilizer for the carrots and onions. 'Besides, why would thieves dig for bones? I don't believe a word of it.'

'They sell the bones to Amils who use them for black magic. The essence of melted bone can be used to control other people.'

'Amils?'

'Yes. Sorcerers who sell talismans and potions to make their living.'

Sharmeen gulped hard. Aziz smiled and shook her head. 'And now you will be scared to sleep in your room again! I am mad to tell you such stories. Can you do me a favour and take these old sheets away? I will wash them tomorrow morning.'

'Of course,' said Sharmeen, picking up the sheets and scurrying out of the room.

***

Aliya opened the door to check on her mother. She seemed to have gone into a fitful sleep.

Walking into Sharmeen's room, she saw that her bed was unmade—Aziz had probably started on it when her mother had screamed and collapsed. She bent down and began to tuck the ends of the sheet into the edge of the mattress. Pulling the duvet back, she noticed a broken bangle at the foot of the bed. She picked up a piece and examined it. It was made of cheap, ochre-coloured glass, speckled with bits of copper, the same shade as Sharmeen's hair. She looked at the remaining pieces, which were arranged in neat little semi-circles, as if an artist had nicked little ripples on a white lake. She picked up the jagged glass and examined it. It had been snapped deliberately into small shards.

She picked up the pieces one by one and then threw them in the wastepaper basket. Sharmeen did have the deplorable habit of picking up feathers and leaves and putting them in her side-table drawer. It was similar to what Aliya herself had done when she was Sharmeen's age, wandering in the garden, rescuing squirrel's babies and fallen sparrows and stray kittens and adopting them. Aziz had followed her around while she did this and they had created their private little zoo. She smiled at the memory and examined the broken pieces. If her mother saw them, she'd have a fit. In her world they signalled the end of a life: a prelude to death by fire, as it had been in the ancient days when a woman lost her husband and broke her bangles, walking over them in penance for becoming a widow; wailing at her destiny before jumping into the funeral pyre to join her man in the afterlife. Broken glass, like death, was a permanent thing.

Aliya shook off the superstition—a bangle was just a bangle. Better to throw the pieces away and not let Amma see them at all.

She picked the last piece and a little shard of glass pierced her index finger, making her wince. Aliya tried to squeeze it out with her nails but that made her finger throb with pain. She decided to let it be. Her body would expel it naturally, the skin would grow underneath and push the glass out in time. It would sort itself out soon.

***

Nani remained in a stupor for the rest of the day, shaking her head, groaning as if she were experiencing a horrible nightmare. Sharmeen watched helplessly, wiping her forehead now, speaking softly to her, thinking that maybe the doctor should be summoned after all. When night began to descend, Aliya came in and took her hand. 'It's almost time for dinner, baby. Eat and go to bed, I'll look after her.' Sharmeen, who was exhausted, obeyed. She bent down to give her grandmother a kiss, and just as she did, Nani opened her eyes.

'Is it time, my moon?' she asked Sharmeen, like a little child.

'It's time for you to sleep, Nani. I'm going to bed too, and I'll see you tomorrow morning. Amma will be here to take care of you,' whispered Sharmeen, tucking wisps of white hair behind her grandmother's ear.

Something changed in Nani's demeanour. The fear receded and she looked at her daughter and frowned. 'No, I will not sleep. Sharmeen, help me up.'

'What? Where are you going?'

'I will eat with you.'

'That's not a good idea, Amma,' said Aliya. 'You need to rest.'

'I am not a weakling like you. I don't need to be sent off to bed the moment something upsets me,' Nani snapped, propping herself up on the bed. 'Give me my cane.'

Sharmeen bounded off the bed and gave it to her, offering her hand for support, which was waved away.

'No. I am not so old that I can't manage on my own.'

Sharmeen pulled her hand away and watched her grandmother walk out of the door, slowly, but with newly found resolve. Aliya stood aside, giving her way. 'The two of you will stay well behind.'

'Nani...'

'*Listen* to me for once. Do not test my patience.'

Sharmeen held back, looking at her mother for some explanation, but Aliya too was mystified at her mother's behaviour. Nani walked slowly down the long hall that led to the dining room at the other end of the house. She stopped when she saw Aziz who was about to announce that dinner was served. She motioned Aliya and Sharmeen to move back away from her.

'Ah Aziz. You are here,' she said, her voice laced with the saccharine tinge of sarcasm.

'Yes, Begum Sahib. Are you well enough to eat? I have laid dinner on the table.'

'Oh ho, very kind of you. So much trouble you go through for us.' Aliya and Sharmeen, who had begun following her, stopped when Nani looked at them and yelled, 'Both of you step back!'

Aliya was about to protest, but Sharmeen pulled her away; Nani had that determined glint in her eye, which meant she expected nothing short of immediate obedience. Arguing would only upset her further.

Satisfied, Nani turned to face Aziz, who stood trembling before her. 'We must thank our Aziz for all he does. Cooking, cleaning, laying the food on the table. Tell me Aziz, is crow's meat on the menu?'

Aziz stiffened. 'I don't know what Begum Sahib means.'

'Begum Sahib is referring to the bird that you butchered and mounted in the garden!' Nani snapped, walking towards him, leaning heavily on her cane with each step she took.

'The crows had been pulling at the grass for their nests. The only way to stop them is to kill one of them as an example to the other crows.'

'An example. Our Aziz now wants to make *an example* of things. Who gave you the authority? You know my rules: No living creature on my property is to be harmed. Yet you killed that crow. And placed it in the space where my granddaughter played?'

Aziz remained quiet.

'And how did you break the talisman? What foul crime did you commit?'

Aziz looked across the hall at Aliya. 'I don't know what Begum Sahib is saying...'

'Don't play innocent. What spells have you performed? Who is it you want to kill? Me, or my daughters?'

Aziz stiffened. From where Sharmeen stood, it seemed as if it was taking all his effort to restrain himself from attacking Nani.

'Don't pretend I don't know what you are!' Nani hissed. She grit her teeth and spat out her words like whiplashes. 'From the minute my husband brought you into this house, I knew there was something wrong about you, something vile and disgusting. Yet I didn't send you away,' she paused, her face wrinkling in contempt at the lanky, slouched creature trembling before her. 'I tolerated your presence around us, until you forgot your place. Isn't it convenient that Amir is in a coma? Aziz can take over again, hold Aliya's hand again, and no one but Begum Sahib can stop him.'

'Amma, what are you saying?' Aliya shouted, shocked at her mother's outrageous accusations.

'You be quiet, silly girl, thinking he's family when all he ever was was vile scum.' Nani focused her narrowed eyes at Aziz and enunciated every word with a terrible deliberation, making sure that each taunt reached its mark. 'And you repay my tolerance with *this*! How many fantasies have you had about my daughter? How many times have you plotted against me? Did you think of me when you killed that crow? Did you enjoy wringing its neck? Filthy, useless spawn of the devil that you are...'

'STOP!' Aziz bellowed, his eyes blazing with clear hatred. His angry voice echoed off the walls and ricocheted against the ceiling. The roof seemed to groan from the impact of his shout. White powder fell to the ground a split second before a big slab of cement dislodged itself from the wooden beam in the ceiling. Sharmeen watched its descent in horror until, with a heavy thud, it came crashing down on Nani's slim frame, crushing her skull and the rest of her body under its weight. Blood spattered on the hallway, against the picture frames. Sharmeen screamed and launched herself towards her grandmother, but Aliya wrenched her back as another portion of the beam followed and fell on top of the dead woman. A cloud of dust made Sharmeen cough and when it cleared, she saw shock and horror on Aziz's face. It was the last thing she remembered before the darkness engulfed her.

Chapter 7

Sharmeen opened Nani's closet and stuck her head in: it still smelled of the rose-scented attar that her grandmother applied so liberally on her clothes—warm, heady and slightly sharp. If only she could resurrect Nani by inhaling hard enough. But her grandmother had been buried a month ago to the caws of crows and the melodic hoot of the koel's lament. And Sharmeen had not even been able to say goodbye.

Nani's funeral had been chaotic. People Sharmeen hadn't known pulling her in one direction and another; incense burning and tamarind seeds clicking; the hum of prayers for the departed soul: that's all she remembered. Sharmeen had fainted after the roof had collapsed and when she awoke, she'd learnt that her grandmother's body had already been taken to be bathed and buried. It had all been done quickly. She'd protested angrily: 'But I didn't get to say goodbye! You should have waited! I didn't get to see her!'

All Aliya had done was shake her head and draw her close, rocking her back and forth while far away, Nani was lowered into the ground.

Sharmeen took her head out of Nani's closet. She felt cheated. Aziz had thought it prudent to bury her immediately because Nani's skull had been crushed and her face mutilated; it was cruel to let anyone see her in that state. 'You can imagine her as she was, strong and smiling at you,' he had told Sharmeen.

But who was Aziz to decide when Nani could be buried? She needed to say goodbye, and Aziz had denied her that.

The roof was repaired by sleepy-looking men who plodded in and out of the house in the days following the funeral. The contractor said that termites had eaten away at the wooden beams between the slabs, and the rafters needed some buttressing, as did the ridge boards. The house was old, and wood could only survive the elements for so long. It had been unfortunate that Begum Sahib had stood under the weakest spot. But when it's time to go, it's time to go.

She now sat in Nani's rocking chair and pushed hard with her heels. It lurched back and swung forward and she kicked again, trying to shake the rising hysteria out of her. Maybe Nani had been right about him. Maybe Aziz was the one who had killed her.

Stupid Aziz.

Stupid Aziz.

Stupid Aziz.

With every rock of the chair, she chanted this mantra in her head. But it didn't make her feel better. She felt her heart beat wildly and braced herself for the violence of tears that came like a thunderstorm, leaving her spent. After she cried, she felt numb, and numbness gave way to niggling guilt. Aziz had been so supportive at a time when she and her mother had been shocked into helplessness. He'd been everywhere at once, taking care of all the possible details, doing all the little things that needed to be done to organize a funeral, clearing up later and putting the house back in order.

Aliya had collapsed when the men returned from Nani's burial. She had drawn a deep breath, the way a child sucks in his pain before belting it out to the world. She'd turned red and Aziz had exclaimed, 'She can't breathe!' Women had crowded around Aliya and Sharmeen stared at her mother helplessly, terrified that she too would die. Aziz rushed in, telling everyone to make room for her. He'd sprinkled water on her face and made her sit up. After breathing resumed, a groan tore itself from the depths of her body as she rocked back and forth, moaning, 'My Amma! Aziz, my Amma!' She was put to bed and Doctor Nawaz prescribed some sleeping pills to calm her nerves.

'Too much for one woman to bear,' he said, patting Sharmeen on the head. 'A daughter to take care of, a husband in a coma and now the death of her mother... Allah have mercy on this family.'

Sharmeen had slipped in the bed beside Aliya as Aziz escorted the doctor to his car. The pulse on her mother's neck throbbed steadily, a small sign of life that was infinitely reassuring. But Aziz came back and told Sharmeen to let

Aliya rest. She had protested as he insisted she sleep in her own room; but he told her not to worry, that all would be well after a good night's sleep.

All had not been well. Nani had not come back. Amma stared into the distance all the time and had to be coaxed to eat. She didn't even visit Abba any more, she just lay in bed sleeping and waking.

Sharmeen craved a miracle. She went to her father's bed and curled herself around him, careful not to crush him. She lay there sobbing for a while, but here too, Aziz interfered.

'Bibi, what are you doing here? Be careful not to bruise Sahib!' Aziz's voice broke her reverie.

'I am being careful!' she snapped.

'Yes, Bibi, I know. It is difficult for you. Come, let Aziz Bhai take you to your room.'

Reluctantly, she obeyed. 'Aziz Bhai, I'm going to sleep with my mother tonight.'

He put a firm hand on her shoulder. 'The doctor said that she should not be bothered; she will be sick if she wakes up in the middle of the night because of some disturbance.' He steered Sharmeen in the direction of her room.

'I won't disturb her! I just don't want to be alone.'

'Who says you are alone? Isn't Aziz Bhai with you? Don't worry Bibi, this is a difficult time and it will pass. Then happiness will come, you will see. Now, climb into bed. Good girl.'

'Why does she sleep all the time?'

'Because the doctor says her nerves are fragile. The

more she rests, the better she will get. Remember: call *me* if you need anything.'

Sharmeen gave him a mutinous look. He looked positively grim—like a cadaver—yet he didn't look exhausted. No, his eyes shone brightly and he no longer slouched as he did when Nani had been alive.

His face was a dark shadow against the light of the corridor. 'Remember, Bibi, you must sleep here from now on.'

Chapter 8

If there is anything worse than misery, it is misery coupled with heat and humidity. The house seemed to wilt in the horrible summer that held it hostage. Sadness and sweat were Sharmeen's constant companions—movement was like wading through a pool of water to get from one place to the next. Flowers drooped, blossoms shrivelled up and even the birds went silent, conserving their energy.

It wasn't just the heat that troubled her. Aziz's increasing possessiveness towards Aliya meant that she did not get to spend any time with her mother. Perhaps different people reacted differently to calamity—some, like Aziz, were filled with the zeal of renewed purpose while others, like her mum, gave up. Her entire body drooped, even the corners of her mouth seemed unwilling to lift into a smile. Aziz buzzed around her, so efficient and eager in his ministrations that it was annoying to witness. Her mother had broken down and Aziz was delightedly picking up the pieces. That was what Nani would have said about the current situation.

Sharmeen felt a quiet anger towards her mum. She didn't see how staying in bed and not doing anything was going to make anything better. She wondered whether happiness would ever return. All the future seemed to hold was empty rooms, sleeping women and oxygen machines.

Tonight she lay awake in her room. It had been miserable at school that day: She hadn't understood her sums and the teacher had made her stand for an hour to shame her into comprehension. After that, half the class hadn't completed their geography lesson, so they were made to stand with their arms raised in the courtyard in the full glare of the afternoon sun. Yousuf, a boy who sat behind her, whispered that the geography ma'am was especially angry because her husband had left her for a younger woman, but the teacher had caught him whispering and so he and Sharmeen were made to stand for an extra five minutes after the others had filed back into class. Escaping school, she'd come home to discover there was no electricity because strong winds had torn the power lines. It was now dark and hot and the silence magnified the rapping of the branches at the window. She rolled over to her side and put her pillow over her head, kneading it into her ear, trying to block out the sound. She recalled Nani's words, 'It's an evil tree, my love. You are right to fear it.'

Sharmeen flung the covers off and hissed at the window, 'Shut up! Shut up, shut up!'

But the sound continued, mocking her.

She ran to Nani's room and sat on her chair and rocked back and forth. Fear gripped her chest. She didn't like the dark, but the sound of silence was a relief. The rocking soothed her nerves. Sharmeen closed her eyes and imagined that Nani was still alive, whispering on her prayer beads.

I cannot protect you any more, Sharmeen. Your Jinn can. Seek him out.

But sitting here in the dark, alone and vulnerable, the significance of what Nani had said loomed over her. How was one supposed to find one's Jinn? Should she call out to him? What if he didn't answer?

Or worse: What if he did?

Sharmeen didn't think she could handle a booming voice coming out of nowhere. She'd have a heart attack. But then she would die and her problems would be over. It was a win-win situation, really.

She stopped rocking and sat very still, concentrating on the moment, listening to the distant howling of a dog. Opening her eyes, she stared into the darkness.

'A...are you there?' she whispered.

Silence.

'A...a...are you there?' she called out, louder than before.

Silence.

The howling of the wind seemed to grow louder, accompanied by the annoying chirp of a cricket.

'Nani said you'd help me. I need you, please.'

Silence.

The seconds rolled into minutes and nothing happened. Disappointment hit her and Sharmeen broke down. There was nothing there. No one. It had all been a lie. Hot tears trickled down her face. Nani had been crazy. There had been no omen, no pact, no Jinn, no magic; just a mean old lady who had treated Aziz badly. Her mother had been right too: There was no invisible power, just this world that was dark and hot. Nani had died a pointless death, Abba had suffered a pointless accident and now they were just pointlessly holding on. There was nothing more to hope for, no more stories, no more twists; theirs was a tragedy that had already happened. The tale was over and they were to live sadly ever after.

Sharmeen wept, long and hard, curling into the rocking chair, hiding her face in the cushion, trembling with fury and exhaustion. And when the storm was spent, she returned to her bed and fell into a deep sleep, too exhausted to be bothered by the constant tapping at her window.

***

The next evening, Sharmeen procrastinated and doodled in her textbook, drawing a ghost in the isosceles triangle. The afternoon's heat had abated and a cool breeze was blowing, whistling and beckoning from a gap in the window.

The sound made her long for a walk. She slammed her book shut and stood up. A walk was something she *could* take and by God, she would take it. What's more, she would take her mother along. She missed her and if Aziz had a problem with it, he could stuff it. She was her Nani's granddaughter and she would take charge, Jinn or no Jinn. Trigonometry, like the rest of the unpleasant things in life, would still be here after she got back.

She ran across the hall to her mother's room.

'Amma, let's go.'

Aliya, who had been combing her hair, started. 'Go where, beta?'

'For a walk! There's a lovely breeze outside and the sun is hiding behind the clouds and it's close to setting anyway,' she insisted as she snatched the hairbrush from her mother's hands. 'Get up!'

Aliya allowed herself to be pulled by her daughter. She smiled and told her to be patient. 'Let me tie my hair!'

She felt a wave of dizziness as she stood up and grabbed Sharmeen's shoulder for support. The past month had taken its toll on her. The idea of getting some fresh air was appealing, as was the sparkle in her daughter's eyes.

They walked down the driveway and stepped onto the grass when Aziz came bounding after them. 'Aliya Bibi, where are you going? Sharmeen, you should let your mother rest!'

Sharmeen winced. There was something out of place in the way he had addressed her. As if he was the boss of her, calling her Sharmeen and not Sharmeen Bibi. This man, who had deprived her of her last goodbye to Nani, was monopolizing her mother and had no right to talk to her as if she was his errant ward.

Sharmeen turned around and said, 'I was taking Amma for a walk, Aziz.'

Aziz. Not Aziz Bhai.

That was deliberate. He needed to be put in his place. A dark cloud passed over Aziz's face and he grit his teeth, but only for a moment. His smile returned, pleading with Aliya, 'Aliya Bibi, Doctor Sahib has asked you to rest. Do you think you should be walking?'

Aliya looked torn. She wanted to walk, but she didn't want to offend Aziz. After all, if she collapsed again, he would have to take care of her. 'Just for a few minutes, Aziz, if you don't mind?'

Sharmeen bristled at the request for permission. Why couldn't her mother just tell Aziz to go away and let her do as she pleased?

She pulled her mother onto the lawn and they took their slippers off, feeling the soft grass beneath their feet, thick like a cushion, somewhat ticklish. It soothed their nerves and they began to stroll, not looking back to see Aziz return to the kitchen.

Ten minutes later, Aliya needed to sit down. She was out of breath, unused to this kind of exertion.

'Amma, you're too weak. You need more exercise.'

'I know. It's the medicines, I think. They make me so sleepy all the time.'

'How long do you have to take them?'

'As long as Doctor Nawaz says I must.'

'But that could be *forever*!' Sharmeen exclaimed, alarmed.

'No, silly! Just for a little while, until I'm stronger.'

'But you can't even walk without panting.'

'The pills soothe my nerves. I get these thoughts that tire me out and I need to rest my mind.'

'What thoughts?'

'Never mind.'

'Tell me. What thoughts make you want to sleep all the time?'

'You're too young.'

'No, I'm not!'

'Don't argue!'

'I *will* argue!' Sharmeen stood up and glared at her mother. 'You pretend like you're the only one who's suffering. But *my* Abba is in a coma, *my* Nani has died and *you* won't spend any time with me. You've not helped me, I'm helping myself. That makes me a grown-up and I want you to talk to me like you'd talk to Abba and tell me what's wrong. Now!'

Aliya teared up and she held her arms out and Sharmeen flung herself into them, curling up into her lap, still very much a child who was terribly alone. 'Nani was right to call me weak. That's exactly what I am.'

'Amma, you need to face whatever it is you're running from. That's what Nani used to say, isn't it?'

'Nani. Yes. She was so proud of you. She used to come alive every time you entered the room. You were her joy, her baby. But I was not.' Aliya's eyes clouded over. 'I fought with her, I argued with her...I...I was sometimes afraid of her. But I loved her too, Sharmeen. I loved her too, and I didn't get to tell her that. But then how could I have?' she asked bitterly.

'Amma, Nani said something to me the day she died.'

'What, baby?'

Sharmeen paused to think. She remembered her

grandmother's warning not to tell her mother about the Jinn or the omen or the spell. Even though Sharmeen was now sure none of it was true, she didn't want to disobey her last wishes. 'Nani said that we had to be careful, that after her, you and Abba and I would be in grave danger.'

Aliya snorted and drew away the strands of hair that the breeze had blown into her eyes. Her hands had aged, looking almost skeletal, veins protruding prominently from them. 'Danger. Always the same thing, even at the end. She should have been more original.' She stared into the distance, scowling. Suddenly, she started.

'I want to go inside.'

'But the weather is so cool! Can't we walk for a little while?'

'No...I...I need my medicine. It's happening again.'

Sharmeen was alarmed by the look of panic on her mother's face. 'Amma, what are you talking about? What's happening?'

'It comes all of a sudden, baby. In waves, so I can't breathe. Like I'll drown. Call Aziz.'

Sharmeen obeyed and yelled for him, holding her mother's shoulders, wanting to comfort her, but not knowing how. Aziz came running up to them.

'How pale you are, Aliya Bibi. Didn't I tell you to rest? Come with me. No, Sharmeen, you've done enough. It's time for Bibi's medicine. Then she'll be fine.'

Sharmeen stared at them, broken, a mosquito buzzing around her head, and the dusk of twilight descending upon the golden afterglow of the evening. She sat for a long time with bowed head, her narrow shoulders drooping and her thick braid hanging limply down her back. To a creature floating in the distance, she looked like a lonely little wisp of a thing, valiantly trying to carry the weight of the world on her shoulders.

She was about to get up and head back towards the house when she noticed a little light hovering above the gulmohar flowers—making them look like red coals. It was a firefly.

'Odd,' she mused. One didn't usually see fireflies in the garden here. There were geckos and rats and butterflies (that looked like moths), pigeons, cockroaches, crickets and frogs (that croaked like someone was farting in the distance), but nothing as lovely and ephemeral as a firefly.

Sharmeen stood up on the bench and tried to reach the creature, but it darted away. She jumped up, swung her arms in the air, but it drifted higher still. Fascinated, she began to climb the tree—which was easy because its branches were low and sturdy. Her eyes were fixed on the firefly, which hovered above, flitting in and out of the flowers, creating a display of orange, crimson and maroon. It was enchanting. She crawled along a branch carefully, testing its weight, hoping it wouldn't break. Holding on with her legs, she sat up, held her hand out and waited. It slowly floated towards her and hovered above her palm.

'You are so beautiful,' she whispered, entranced.

'Why, thank you!'

Sharmeen blinked and came out of her stupor.

'Funny, I thought you just talked to me,' she chuckled.

The firefly glowed brightly in the dark. 'Yes. That's because I *did* talk to you.'

Her heart slammed against her chest and she screamed and fell off the tree, the branches scraping her arms and legs and she closed her eyes, sure that she was going to crack her skull. A familiar buoyancy held her a smack second before she made contact. She hovered above the ground before being gently laid on the grass. Sharmeen opened her eyes. The branches of the gulmohar swayed in the background and the firefly glowed over her eyes.

'You really need to be more careful, Sharmeen,' it said in a thick baritone.

Letting out another terrified yelp, she shot up and ran inside, past Aziz who asked her what the matter was, past her mother's bedroom, past her own into her grandmother's room and scooted under the covers, frightened out of her mind.

Chapter 9

'Bibi? Is everything okay?' Aziz enquired from the doorway.

Sharmeen nodded under the covers and said, in a strangled voice, 'I'm playing a game, Aziz.'

'A game? By yourself?'

'Yes.'

'Does Bibi need a partner? I can play with you.'

'No. I'm fine. Leave me alone.'

She heard him sigh and walk out. Her mind whirled as she tried to process what she had just experienced. She had been sad—she had seen a firefly—she'd climbed the tree—and had fallen off, but been airborne. And then the firefly had told her to be careful. Hallucinations. She'd injured her head. There was probably internal bleeding.

But she felt fine. Sharmeen lay still, her hands grabbing fistfuls of the bedcover and clutching it over her body as she trembled. She reviewed the episode in her mind again. The firefly had spoken. Oh God, yes, it had spoken before she'd fallen. And she hadn't fallen. She'd been carried down. And the voice that spoke to her on the ground was the same voice that spoke to her on the tree.

Which meant that she hadn't gone mad after the fall, she'd gone mad before it.

The covers no longer smelt of Nani's attar—they'd been washed by Aziz—yet another reminder removed. Sharmeen couldn't breathe properly anymore, so she stuck her head out and thought about the firefly. It had talked to her. Therefore, it was no ordinary firefly.

So Nani's stories had not been nonsense. And that meant that her great-great-great grandmother had indeed walked among the gulmohars at maghrib time and had met her Jinn. Which meant that this firefly too was a...

Sharmeen shuddered again, but this time excitement tinged her fear. If her Jinn was trying to communicate with her, it meant that there was someone to help her. She looked out of the window, where the golden and pink hues of the day seemed to dispel the gloom of the grey room. She needed to go back outside—to face her fear and her Jinn.

She got out of bed and splashed her face with cold water before treading back to the garden. Her heart thumped hard against her ribs as she approached the gulmohar. She didn't relish the idea of a firefly or something else jumping out at her. She tiptoed towards the roots of the tree and wrapped her arms around herself, looking up at its flowers. It seemed like a normal tree. And then she saw it again, hovering over the flowers.

She cleared her throat and summoned the courage to call out. The first attempt was a strangled whisper. She cleared her throat again and said, in a tremulous voice, 'Hello.'

The firefly didn't respond, though it hovered in one spot, waiting.

Sharmeen closed her eyes. 'Hello!' she said again, with a little more confidence.

'Hello,' came the same deep voice.

She backed away and stifled a scream.

'You know, this is getting tedious. Make up your mind. Do you want to talk to me or should I go? I have better things I could be doing.'

Blinking at the unexpected scolding that reminded her of Nani's impatience, Sharmeen rallied. 'A...are...are you my Jinn?' she asked, her eyes wide.

'Well, I don't know about being *your* Jinn, but yes, I am a Jinn. I am on your side though, if that's what you mean.'

Sharmeen noticed that every time the voice came, the glow became brighter.

'P-please don't hurt me.'

'Tell me, how much damage do you think a small firefly can do to a human girl?'

Sharmeen took a moment to try and picture that.

'Th-thank you for breaking my fall.'

The firefly swept in closer. 'You're quite welcome.'

'C-can we just sit here quietly until I get used to this... used to you, I mean?'

'Of course. I shall be hovering over here, glowing as usual.'

Sharmeen sat on the bench and eyed the firefly-who-was-a-Jinn warily, for what must have been twenty minutes, watching it glow brighter as the sky above it grew darker. She decided to brave a bit of conversation.

'Are you a firefly?'

'Well, I'm currently in the form of one.'

'I...I don't understand.'

'What's to understand?'

'Um...that, you...you're a Jinn, but you are a firefly as well.'

'Ah!' came the voice, 'I understand your dilemma. Well, I am a Jinn you see, but past experience has taught me that unpleasant things tend to happen if I make my presence known suddenly. Some people faint, some soil their pants. Women are particularly prone to shrill shrieks. Men launch their slippers at me, sometimes they fire pistols—depending on whatever is at hand. Others yelp and run away, as you have so aptly demonstrated in the past hour.'

Sharmeen hung her head low, feeling sheepish.

'Therefore, in the attempt to avoid homicide and general violence, I try and appear in some form of harmless disguise, to ease the shock. Which is why I hover before you as a firefly.'

'What is your name?'

'Oh, you won't be able to pronounce my real name. If you try to speak in my language, you'll sound like you're trying to whistle, gargle and howl all at once—which, of course, is something your epiglottal efforts will never be able to achieve.'

'Why not?'

'Can you cough and sneeze at the same time?'

'I've never tried it.'

'Because you can't. My real name is unpronounceable to humans; since I come before you as a firefly, you may call me Jugnu.'

Sharmeen nodded and began to stand up. The firefly flew back to give her some space. She was less afraid now and a thousand questions flooded her mind.

'You're here?' she asked, somewhat inanely.

'It appears that I am. But that has already been established.'

'I called for you. With a prayer on my grandmother's tasbeeh.'

'So you did,' came the cheerful reply.

'So you are the Jinn I created?' Sharmeen asked eagerly.

'I most certainly am *not*,' Jugnu said indignantly. 'There is but one Creator and I serve Him, just like you. But yes, you did call for me when you recited the prayer on the beads. And since you are the human I've been paired up with, I came as soon as I could.'

'Paired up with?'

'Well, you know how it goes with our collective history, don't you? Humzaads? Twin Jinn et al?'

Sharmeen shook her head.

'You don't? You mean you haven't heard of the one man-one Jinn policy?'

Sharmeen shook her head.

'Oh. Well. I shall have to explain. You see, God created

us in pairs, one human for every Jinn, and divided us by an invisible curtain that humans cannot cross, but Jinn can. So I am your Jinn and you are my man. Well, sort of. But you haven't created me, any more than I have created you. Have you heard of kindred spirits?'

'Yes!'

'Well, you and I are sort of like that. You could say that I am your spirit, but that makes me sound like your pet, which isn't something I take kindly to. But we are linked because we were created together.'

'Do all humans know about this, Jugnu? Because I certainly didn't.'

'Some do. The stupid ones don't.'

'I thought men were paired up with women in heaven. That's what my Islamiat teacher taught me at school.'

'Well, she's wrong. Men are physical creatures: visible and concrete, destructive and creative, populating this earth. But we Jinn are invisible, and while we are no less destructive or creative, we are a little wiser for the wear. It's because we can still occasionally listen to the angels and God—something that stopped for humans a long time ago. So we're not as confused, you see. This places us in an excellent position to help you whenever you've gone astray.'

Sharmeen listened, fascinated. She was no longer afraid. Jugnu sounded so normal, so *familiar*. 'So you are my guardian angel.'

'No, please! Angels are the dullest creatures imaginable. All they do is pray-obey-pray-obey. No sense of humour. Jinn have a lot more personality. And while I'll try to help you, Sharmeen, remember, the only person who can help you is yourself. I'm not anyone's saviour.'

'I see,' said Sharmeen, a little crushed. 'I just thought, because you said that God had created a Jinn for every one of us, that you would all be there to help us.'

'Which is a typically human, self-centred manner of thinking.'

Sharmeen blinked, realizing she had been snubbed. She opened her mouth to argue but then closed it. It didn't seem wise to pick a fight with a Jinn.

'Man has always believed himself to be superior to us. It's the same argument over and over again—*you were supposed to bow down to Adam. We are your superiors—God willed it so.* As if bowing down is the same thing as an acceptance of inferiority.'

'Isn't it?'

'No, it was an acknowledgment of existence, nothing more, nothing less. Just as we are in a position to help man, man is in a position to help us. It is by helping those we can easily destroy that we are able to maintain what is good and true in us. We are made of fire, and fire can destroy as well as create. Some of our kind opted to destroy the men they were meant to help. And in doing so, they wreaked havoc in their own souls.'

'Jinn have souls?'

'No, we have snub noses. *Of course* we have souls. We're almost the same as you. Except invisible. And with a less limited imagination, might I add.'

Sharmeen thought about it for a moment. The story her

teacher had told her in class had certainly been different: that man was the centre of the universe because God had made him so, and the Jinn were eternally jealous and therefore had wanted to take revenge.

'Satan was a Jinn too, wasn't he?'

'Unfortunately.'

'And he was paired up with Adam? They were kindred spirits?'

'No, no, no. He was just asked to bow before him, which of course, he didn't, giving our kind a bad reputation forever. He disobeyed. And then Adam came into this world and was lost. But that's when the system of pairing began—and God sent no one less than Maraj to guide Adam out of the wilderness.'

'Who's Maraj?'

'The first of Jinn, born sixty thousand years before Adam was ever created. It was apt—the first of Jinn helping out the first of men. It's all very interesting; we were taught all this as babies.'

Babies. Oddly, there was something comforting in the fact that Jinn were once babies too. It made them seem more human. Sharmeen thought about this before another question came to her mind.

'So, men and Jinn have been paired up from before we were born?'

'Yes. They have.'

'How long have you been with me, Jugnu?'

'Since the day you fell down while playing hopscotch.'

Sharmeen crinkled her brow.

'You mean when I, sort of, flew instead of falling?'

'Yes, though it would be a stretch to say you flew. I merely blocked you and laid you down to safety, as soft as a feather. As I did just now. You do have a tendency to take some nasty falls.'

'But...why then, Jugnu? Why didn't you show yourself sooner?'

'Because you had no need of me until then.'

'Last night, I called for you, in my room. You didn't come then either.'

'I did indeed. Didn't you hear the cricket? Well, that was me. I was chirping in Morse code, I'll have you know. I was hoarse by the end of it, but then I realized that they've probably stopped teaching Morse in schools. And then you went back to sleep. I couldn't be more obvious, you see, for the same reasons: I say hello, you scream, the house awakes and there's a disaster over nothing. This was a good time to catch you alone, with you here by yourself in the open, to prevent a scene. A firefly is a very pretty creature, but it belongs outside. I can change myself into a butterfly, but what would you have done to a butterfly in your room in the dead of night? Is it at all natural?'

'No,' Sharmeen agreed, 'But then this isn't natural either!'

'Now I'm hurt,' said Jugnu, sitting on Sharmeen's knee. 'It's a breezy evening and we're alone, surrounded by these beautiful red flowers. You screamed but that's to be excused—you're young—and you came back. We're conversing like we've been good friends for ages. I'd say it was a beautifully orchestrated affair.'

'Well, if you put it like that, yes, this is much better than a butterfly at midnight,' agreed Sharmeen.

'Or a voice in the dark,' said Jugnu, 'or a dwarf in the corner of a house. I once did that to a woman—stood behind the door of her kitchen. She threw a knife at me. Terrible aim thankfully.'

One thought in particular kept flitting about in Sharmeen's mind.

'Jugnu, Nani used to say Jinn possess people. A-are you going to, I mean...is that what you plan to do?'

The firefly glowed brightly as Jugnu answered with tired resignation, 'You humans are obsessed with possession. As if it's something that Jinn love to do. Let me tell you something, possession is hard work and downright exhausting. Plus I'll have you know, some people are awful to possess. I once occupied a man with terrible body odour—I had nightmares of over-ripe guavas for years after that. Besides, I have no reason to possess you. And of course, I can't possess you even if I wanted to.'

'Why not?'

'Because you are still an innocent. You have not bled. Only with the onset of puberty does possession become possible. And since most possession is done by the Undesirables amongst us Jinn, they are especially attracted to the smell of...you know, fertility. The rest of us would like to avoid it as much as we can. It's a vile thing to do and I have a healthy respect for my personal space, which as you can imagine, is out of the question during the process.'

'I see,' said Sharmeen, lost in thought.

'But worry not, I have no desire to possess you. I am here because you need my help.'

'Yes, I do. Jugnu, if you've been with me, you've seen what's happened. My grandmother has died and she told me to beware of Aziz.'

'Yes, he's a singularly odd fellow. I've been observing him. More to him than what meets the eye.'

'But I don't know where the danger comes from. I don't know how to help Amma. I don't know how to protect my father and I don't know how to make everything better. Can you help me?'

Jugnu glowed thoughtfully for a moment. 'I can use some of my powers to unearth a few of the mysteries, certainly.'

'What powers do you have?' asked Sharmeen.

'Oh, the standard things available to all invisible spirits: fly, push people and things around. Listen in on private conversations. Feel emotions, sometimes hear thoughts. And of course, I can travel from one end of the world to the other in a matter of seconds.'

'How amazing!' said Sharmeen, clapping her hands. 'Can you make me fly too?'

Jugnu flew up and sat on the tip of her nose. 'Look at my size. I might be able to help one of your eyelashes fly. The rest of you is too heavy!'

Sharmeen laughed, throwing her head back, dislodging Jugnu from his seat at the end of her nose. She had thought that meeting a Jinn would be devastating. She had expected a fearsome creature with sharp claws, angry fangs and red eyes. She had expected fear, panic, devastation, anything except this gentle flow of energy warming her through, making her think that with this particular twist in the tale, things might be alright after all. Although a new thought lined her newfound happiness with an edge of panic.

'Jugnu,' she asked, 'What do you really look like?'

'Why do you want to know, little one?'

'Because I don't like disguises, Jugnu. You can see me as I really exist. I want to know what a Jinn looks like.'

'You will not be able to see me, Sharmeen. There is a curtain between us; I cannot make you see me even if I wanted to. That is why I must take the shape of creatures that are visible to the human eye.'

'But surely you can *describe* what you're like?' Sharmeen insisted.

'Well, can you imagine what air would look like?'

'It's, well...air is thin, and everywhere. But it's all around.'

'Yes, little one. It's tiny enough to fit in your nostrils, or occupy an entire desert. You can think of me like that—a hurricane that can be huge enough to topple a building, but also small enough to be inhaled by a human, giving me access to his brain, like encephalitis. That's an unfortunate simile, wonder how that popped into my mind! Never mind. Forget I said it.'

'You can topple a building?'

'I can, but I can't say I've ever done it. But I do love destroying billboards and things during a storm. It's great fun—especially if they've been put there illegally.'

'But I can feel air when it moves. If you move, Jugnu, will I be able to feel you?'

'If I rush through you, yes. But we should first get to know each other a little better, don't you think, little one?'

'I suppose so. *I* don't mind,' Sharmeen hinted. 'But if you don't think it's appropriate, perhaps another time.' She looked down at her hands and pursed her lips in feigned disappointment, the way she used to whenever she wanted to make her father change his mind about something.

The firefly seemed to droop—it hung low and its tiny legs seemed to grow longer and limper. Jugnu let out a loud sigh.

'Close your eyes. This will take a moment.'

Sharmeen obeyed. She felt a rush of air on her forehead and a feeling of languid warmth flooded her body. It felt like a cold breeze, and she saw the vision of a high mountain overlooking a verdant forest. She saw the sun, the colour of golden honey, rise from distant ranges, grey and sombre in their majesty. Its rays kissed the top of the trees with their light. She felt peace and calm; cupped like a bee snuggled in a yellow buttercup, sheltered and protected.

'Jugnu, you're wonderful!' she exclaimed.

'Thank you. Very kind.'

The moment faded and the sound of a buzzing mosquito brought her back to the reality of the evening. She opened her eyes in the dark—there was no firefly to be seen.

She heard a whisper: 'I must go now, but don't worry, I'll be close.'

Sharmeen wanted to tell him to come back, but she was interrupted by the sound of Aziz's voice.

'Bibi, what are you doing here in the dark? Come inside.'

Sharmeen stared at the cluster of red flowers on the gulmohar: there was no firefly among them. She got up and followed Aziz inside, but the despair and desolation that she had felt since Nani's death were now gone and hope filled the void. She was no longer afraid.

Chapter 10

When she was six, Sharmeen got herself stuck in a kiddie slide, unable to move, her hips firmly wedged in. Her father watched her wriggle and squirm, trying his best not to laugh. But when she called out 'Abba, help me!' he'd hooted and guffawed, stopping only when she threatened that she wouldn't be his daughter anymore.

Sharmeen smiled at the memory early this morning, as she sat next to his bed, watching him breathe with difficulty. The arms that had swept her off the slide and wrapped her in a bear hug were now brown sticks by his side, and the paunch which she loved to bury her face in had disappeared. He was a sleeping wraith, eyes permanently closed.

The memories were growing more distant—that was what upset her the most. Like the time when he'd walked in on her eating toothpaste in the bathroom. 'Amma better not find out,' he'd warned just as Aliya walked in and caught her daughter green-handed. And then he'd blocked his daughter from his wife who threatened to slap the grin right off Sharmeen's face—apparently the seven-year-old had gone through three tubes already. 'Let her be, my love,' he'd said, 'Colgate can be very hard to resist.' Sharmeen frowned: she remembered that was what he said, but she couldn't remember what his voice sounded like. This bothered her immensely.

She touched his fingers, reliving their former excursions when they would walk hand in hand after he returned from work in the early evenings. He'd ask about her day and discuss his. Like Nani, he would also talk to her like she was an adult—never patronizing. They'd go over the books she would be reading—*Adventure Stories for Boys*, *The Antics of Shaikh Chillee*, and *The Giant with Three Golden Hairs*—exchanging notes, with Sharmeen invariably demanding to know why all the exciting stories full of action and adventure were reserved for male protagonists while girls were always sitting at home, sewing clothes and mourning their lost pets or parents. He said it was because people often assumed that little girls needed to be protected and not encouraged to get into dangerous scrapes. Not that he agreed with them. 'Maybe you can grow up and write a book about the grand adventures little girls have,' he'd suggested. And Sharmeen had instantly wished for an adventure to write about.

'I'm in the middle of one now, Abba,' she spoke out loud. 'Why don't you wake up and join me?'

But she received only laboured breathing in response. Her musings were interrupted by Aziz. 'Sharmeen Bibi! You're already awake? You don't have to wake up for another thirty minutes to go to school.'

'I just wanted to spend some time alone with him,' she replied curtly.

'Well, I don't think it's wise to sit so close to him,' he said, untucking the sheet from underneath the mattress to change it.

Sharmeen moved over to the sofa and glared at Aziz mutinously. 'I miss my parents. And you are keeping me away from them.'

Aziz looked up at her, surprised. 'Keeping you away? I don't know what you mean.'

'All you do is tell me to not disturb Amma, to sit away from Abba, as if I were going to hurt them.'

Aziz paused. 'I don't mean to do that. But isn't your father fragile? Does his skin not bruise easily?'

'That's not what I...'

'Am I making that up?' he asked gently.

'Yes, he is fragile. But...'

'And your mother is tired. She needs her rest, so that she can be strong enough to take important decisions. Doctor Nawaz told me himself that she needs a lot of sleep to soothe her mind. The walk yesterday drained her.'

'It drained her because she's not getting any exercise!' Sharmeen insisted. 'She should spend her time with me. I can cheer her up!'

Aziz walked up to Sharmeen and placed his hands on her shoulders. Alarm bells went off as she recalled Nani's warning and shrugged his hands away. 'I know what is bothering Sharmeen Bibi. She is lonely.'

She didn't know why, but his tone made her uncomfortable.

'Sharmeen Bibi has also had a shock.' Aziz said. 'She is sad and alone, she misses her Amma and Abba and her grandmother also. Begum Sahib's death was a terrible blow for her.'

Sharmeen felt tears forming, but blinked them away. 'Yes, and I wasn't even there to bury her. I didn't get to say goodbye!'

'Sharmeen Bibi knows that her Nani would have wanted to be buried as soon as possible. Hadn't her grandmother said so countless times while she was alive?'

She wiped the tears from her cheeks. Nani had always believed that when the soul departed, the body longed to be re-united with the earth. Aziz was right, it would have been against Nani's wishes to wait.

'But Sharmeen Bibi has been left alone. And it is Aziz Bhai's fault,' he continued, placing a hand on her shoulder once more. 'Aziz Bhai has been careless. He has been so busy taking care of Aliya Bibi and Amir Sahib that he has given no attention to Sharmeen. It's been so long since we played hopscotch together, or any of the other games we used to play. But I'm so glad that Sharmeen Bibi has talked to him. Don't worry, he will not ignore her anymore.'

Sharmeen frowned.

'Aziz, I'm not a child. I just want to be with my mother.'

But he wasn't listening. His other hand also curled around Sharmeen as he drew her in for a hug. 'Aziz Bhai will be there for his Sharmeen Bibi. I used to carry you every evening, in my arms, so that you would go to sleep. Aliya Bibi told me to stop spoiling you, but I could not.

I still remember the day you were born. I had stood with Amir Sahib outside the operation theatre. He had been so nervous and then you came and he held you in his arms. We were all so happy. We distributed sweets to the entire neighbourhood. I ate the first laddoo in your honour. You know what your father told me when you were born? *You are her second father.'*

A cold chill of warning unfurled in the pit of her stomach. Nani's final accusation reverberated in her mind. *For Aziz to take over again. For Aziz to hold Aliya's hand again, without Begum Sahib to stop him.* And realization struck, as rude as a splash of ice-cold water on a winter's day. 'I have only *one* father, Aziz,' Sharmeen said, pulling away. 'And he's lying over there, sleeping. And he *will* wake up. And then Amma, Abba and I will be a family once again.'

Aziz reached out to draw her into an embrace, but Sharmeen ran out of the room, not looking back to see his fingers curl into a tight fist.

Chapter 11

Sharmeen slipped out into the garden, deep in thought. She couldn't shake off the feeling that Aziz was somehow responsible for Nani's death.

He wanted her to depend on him. But she had to be her own saviour. Where was Jugnu? She sat on the bench and closed her eyes, trying to ignore the voice in her head telling her that yesterday had been a dream; that she had imagined the whole thing. She called out, 'Jugnu? Are you there?'

Nothing happened. No firefly descended.

She swallowed. 'Jugnu? Are you here? Come out, please.'

And on a whiff of wind, she heard a deep whisper, 'Not here. Find another spot.'

Sharmeen got up immediately, relieved. 'Where?'

'Some place where you're not visible from the house.'

She walked over to a high, evergreen shrub that separated the garden from the vegetable patch at the back. She scooted behind and called out, 'Is this okay?'

'Perfectly fine,' came Jugnu's voice, but he was nowhere to be found.

'Where *are* you?'

'Down here. On the ground.'

Sharmeen saw a shiny black beetle with a shovel-like head trundling towards her. Its legs were spindly but long, and they carried a body that seemed to be suited in metallic armour, curving down toward the ground. An upturned horn, like a rhino's, stood arrogantly on its head.

'What are you?'

'I...' Jugnu proclaimed proudly, 'am a dung beetle!'

Sharmeen scooted away when he crawled up near her legs.

'Yuck. Why would you want to be a dung beetle of all things?'

'We Jinn are very impressed with dung beetles.'

'Impressed? Why?' Sharmeen asked, horrified.

'They have excellent taste.' Jugnu was beginning to sound irritated. There was no expression on the beetle's face for Sharmeen to judge if this were true. It looked, well, like a beetle. But it had stopped moving.

'Dung beetles eat dung, Jugnu,' she reminded him.

'Yes, I know. So do Jinn.'

'Oh.'

'Indeed.'

Sharmeen stared at the beetle; it stared back at her. The absurdity of the situation made her giggle.

'Honestly, Jugnu, isn't it the slightest bit *disgusting* that you are a dung beetle right now? After a firefly? And you can't possibly eat dung!'

'Why not?'

'Because it's gross!'

'Oh ho!' said Jugnu, his voice shaking a bit, as if he were really angry. 'Gross, is it? And what about you humans? Eating flesh and unborn foetuses.'

'We don't eat unborn foetuses!' Sharmeen protested.

'Really? What do you think eggs are?'

Sharmeen opened her mouth to answer back, but couldn't say anything. Termed like that, eggs did sound disgusting. Why, she'd eaten an unborn foetus just yesterday. Deep fried.

'What's the matter? Dung beetle got your tongue? You humans kill to eat. We only consume what nature has no more need of. We do not destroy to satisfy our baser needs. In fact, like the noble dung beetle, we crawl in afterwards, roll in the delicacies and feast on them. Lots of protein and methane. It's what gives us energy. You humans are only just now realizing how waste can generate so much power, but we've known it forever. It's why we can lift heavy things and reach the end of the world in a millisecond and back. Enough gas for a space rocket. Super duper master blaster.'

Sharmeen tried to hide her queasiness.

'So...' she said after a while. 'Dung.'

'Yes. Dung.'

'Is there anything else that you eat besides dung?'

'Bones.'

'Bones?'

'Yes. Bones. We suck them dry.'

'Like vampires?'

'No Sharmeen, vampires, according to mistaken human folklore, suck blood. Besides, the vampires that you read of in books, with capes and fangs and sun allergies don't really exist.'

'Of course I knew vampires were just make-believe.'

'Well...the ones you are thinking of certainly are. But creatures like them do exist. The Lyllurian.'

'What are those?'

'A more grammatically correct question would be "Who are they?" They are four Jinn: one sister and her handmaiden, and two brothers, doing the usual sort of stuff—feasting on the dead in graveyards, mesmerizing humans, playing with them for entertainment. Thoroughly unpleasant individuals, but we needn't bother with them: they live near the border between Ukraine and Slovakia, and are therefore not our problem.'

'Ah,' said Sharmeen, thinking how odd it was to be discussing the geographical location of vampires so matter-of-factly. Along with the diet of Jinn. Bones, she said to herself, were not quite as bad as dung. But it was all quite morbid.

'It isn't morbid. You really don't have an open mind, do you?' Jugnu said.

Sharmeen started. 'How...I didn't say anything!'

'I know, but I heard your thoughts!'

'You can do that?'

'Yes. Which is why you can never lie to a Jinn.'

'Oh. So Jinn are mind-readers as well.'

'Well, reading is a misleading term. Your thoughts are

invisible. Technically, so am I. So I can see your thoughts, in images, colours, shapes and sizes.'

Sharmeen was fascinated. 'I didn't realize that my thoughts had colours and dimensions. How interesting.'

'Well, you humans can feel what other people are thinking—if you are intuitive enough. If you're around a mean person, you begin to feel small and cramped, because their thoughts are boring into you. And when you are around someone who wants something from you, then no matter how nice they are, you'll still feel heavy and tired in their presence.'

'That's how I'm feeling with Aziz these days, Jugnu. I think he's cast some kind of spell over Amma, she's completely dependent on him. I know this because he tried to do the same thing with me, but his words didn't affect me for long. I have no idea how he's doing it, but he is. I think Nani was right about him.'

'Of course she was,' said Jugnu, nodding so that the curved horn on his head sliced the air. He dug into a clod of earth and rolled it over, climbing on top. He sniffed it, but lost interest. 'You *really* need fertilizer in this garden of yours.'

Sharmeen ignored the last comment. She had no desire to think any more about what Jugnu ate. 'Did you know my Nani, Jugnu?'

'No, I did not. But I have heard of her. Your Nani was one of the old, wise ones, when humans and Jinn coexisted with a bond of mutual respect and humility. She had great regard for our kind, and in turn was revered by us. Plus, any possessor of the silver beads is a friend of mine.'

Sharmeen crossed her legs and leaned back on her palms, looking up at the sky, where wisps of cloud seemed suspended like tattered rags. 'How come my prayers called *you* specifically, Jugnu? How come someone else didn't come?'

'Because I am your humzaad.'

'But Jugnu, yesterday you said you were created with me.'

'I was created with you, but I have been around a longer time.'

'I don't understand. If you were created with me, then you should be twelve years old!'

'You have an old soul, little one, but a young body. We don't need a body, hence we can enter the world at the point of our creation.'

'How old are you, Jugnu?'

'Oh, I've been around a century, give or take a few years. Fairly youthful by Jinn standards, so don't look so shocked!'

'Sorry. Does that mean I'm a hundred years old?'

'Your soul is.'

Sharmeen suddenly felt very heavy, as if the effect of age was bearing down on her body. Thinking that you were twelve but finding that your soul was a hundred was a lot to process. What did it mean? Is that why her grandmother trusted in her instead of her mother? Is that why she was able to communicate with a Jinn while her mother was not?

'But why wasn't I born a hundred years ago?'

'Because the One above, in His infinite wisdom, saw that you were needed now. You must learn to accept things as they are. We are sent here for a purpose. We find ourselves at a particular junction in time because we have a role to play. Your Nani knew that you have a special destiny and that is why she prepared you when she died. You weren't just a twelve-year-old child to her. You had inherited the blood of her line.'

'Jugnu, are you bound to help me? Is it compulsory?'

'Really, the word "bound" is so tedious. I was created with you, so yes, that makes us close. But that doesn't *force* me to do anything. I value my freedom. I'd much rather roam the highest mountains in the world, but those too have been populated by mountaineers and adventure enthusiasts. Many humans, due to misread religious texts and delusions of grandeur, think that they can summon Jinn to do their bidding. Well, let me clarify that there are no lamps to hold us hostage; we do *not* need to be rubbed out of our residences and we do *not* grant wishes.'

'It would be so much more convenient if you did!' exclaimed Sharmeen, watching the beetle crawl up a blade of grass and plop down on the ground.

'Yes, well, even if we could, all you humans would do is get yourself into further scrapes. Most Jinn don't want to have anything to do with humans: all you do is bicker. It's because you lack space. We don't need a lot of space, considering that we can curl up upon a rose petal or lay claim on a mountain top. That's the benefit of not having a physical body. I could have ignored your plea and been none the worse for it.'

'You mean you don't *want* to help me?' Sharmeen asked in consternation.

'Well, you did make fun of what I ate.'

'I didn't mean to!' protested Sharmeen. 'I was just a bit shocked when you told me, that's all.'

'Learn to take some teasing. Of course I want to help you. You're not half bad. All I'm saying is, I am not bound by some ancient decree of God. I have free will, just like you. But I am also here to honour Morpir, the wise Amluq and son of Samarkand.'

Sharmeen rubbed her eyes, which, to her embarrassment, were wet with tears. She hated melodrama of all sorts and didn't want Jugnu to think she was silly.

'The son of Samarkand? Why would you want to honour him?'

'It's a nasty story.'

'I'd like to hear it.'

'I'd really rather not go into it.'

'Please?'

The beetle came close and Sharmeen stopped herself from drawing back. It curled its legs beneath its armoured frame and sat down—something ordinary dung beetles would never do, she was sure.

'I honour Morpir because I am forever indebted to him. And a Jinn never forgets a favour. I was very foolish when I was young, and heady with my own powers. Humans were weak and oblivious of my presence and this made me feel invincible. I now realize that that was my first test as a Jinn—to have power over the physical world, and to not abuse it. However, thoughts of right and wrong seldom enter a young Jinn's head. It's like being a bully in a playground—you hit and steal and punch just because you can.

'One of my mates and I delighted in tormenting men. He used to take human shape and spread rumours about a haunted museum in the city centre. When people came to see for themselves, I pushed around furniture and shouted and banged until they were terrified out of their minds. It was wildly entertaining, their fear was the reason we lived. Our pastime made us urban legends, and we were thrilled about it.

'One day my friend lured a man into the museum in the middle of the night. I howled and screamed and made five knives fly in his direction. Of course, they missed him narrowly, as was the plan. But what the knives did not accomplish, my shenanigans did. He dropped dead of fright. His heart had stopped.

'I'd only wanted to scare him, not kill him. My friend fled, but I could not just abandon my victim. A few days later, his wife found him and buried him. I was wracked with guilt and didn't know what to do. Killing a creature of God is the worst crime any Jinn can commit. I thought I was doomed to hell. And then one day, my victim's wife brought to the museum a man posing as a sorcerer who claimed to know how to control Jinn.'

'Can men control Jinn?' asked Sharmeen.

'Only a handful in history have ever managed. These have been great men, with strong minds and brave hearts and in their wisdom, they know better than to try and conquer our kind. Jinn cooperate out of love, not coercion.

Force will just end up in disaster. Most try, but in the end, it is the Jinn who destroys the man, because, you see, a trapped Jinn is an angry Jinn and an angry Jinn isn't very comfortable company. This sorcerer, he was not holy, but he had a few tricks up his sleeve. He came to where I was and read verses backwards from the holy book. He slaughtered a chick and a goat and mingled their blood with his own, invoking the names of the Si'ilat, sons of the she-demon Udhrut and her mate Qutrub. I'd never had a human confront me like this, invoking the names of the fearful Jinn; but it was largely ineffectual, because it was all for show to impress the widow. I thought he'd leave, but he took out a crowbar made of meteorite iron, and this, you should know, is a Jinn's kryptonite. I still don't know how he got his hands on it—they usually have counterfeit ones made of ordinary steel that have no effect on us. But meteorite iron is another matter: we hate it. I felt all my power draining away. This sorcerer emptied a small vial and muttered and waved the iron bar all over. I was caught unawares and sucked deep into the vial, just to get away from the damn crowbar. He corked the vial and wrapped it with a sheet, again, from the same stuff as the crowbar. I was trapped. No matter how much I struggled, the cold of the iron struck me like the poison of the most lethal mamba. I was wounded. It was my first encounter with pain. I had to fold and make myself tiny so that I didn't touch the walls of the vial, which would enervate me. This was my punishment.'

'You poor thing,' said Sharmeen, reaching and stroking the beetle on its back. It felt smooth and wet.

'Thank you, but I had driven a man to his death. I deserved it. For two years I remained imprisoned, consumed by guilt and misery. It was ironic—the haunter became the haunted. But this punishment was of my choosing. I could have opted out of it, and the vial very easily, all I had to do was choose the dark way.'

'The dark way?'

'The way of Satan, the first of the Qarins.'

'I don't get it.'

Jugnu sighed. 'Your grandmother has left a lot of holes in your education. When God was turning him out of Heaven, Satan made one request—to be granted the power of the Whisper through which he could tempt mankind to foul deeds. God agreed, but gave it not just to Satan but to all Jinn. We can, if we choose to, drive a man to harm himself and others. If a man is put on this earth to be the best he can be, the Qarins make sure that he is led astray. It's remarkably easy.'

'So you could have whispered to your captor to let you go.'

'Yes, and sometimes I wanted to tell him to free me and set himself on fire. I wanted to hear his screams of agony as he died. But if a Jinn becomes a Qarin, then there's no turning back. He has pledged his allegiance to Satan and will be among the damned. As much as I wanted to get out of my little hell, to become a Qarin meant earning a tiny reprieve in *this* world to endure an eternity of hell. No. I knew that things would not always be the same. I knew I would have to bear my suffering before I was delivered back to the freedom and peace I was born into. Something would change.'

'There would be a twist in the tale,' Sharmeen thought.

'Yes, that's a good way of putting it. My twist came with a man wearing a flowing white robe, looking at me with the bluest of eyes, with vertical pupils like blue almonds— which, by the way, is the classic sign of an Amluq. He offered the sorcerer something priceless, in exchange for possession of the vial.'

'What did he offer?'

'The wail of a child whose parents had been murdered.'

'That's awful, Jugnu! What was Morpir doing with such a thing?'

'Well, Morpir wasn't always the sort who would help the distressed in need. The journey of an Amluq is a terrible one and I have known none other than Morpir to come out of it clean on the other side. If you look carefully, there exist several lost souls that can sometimes manifest as the lonely, homeless, addicted. Now most of them are human, wretches abandoned by society. But some of those are Amluqs in the first stage of their journey. You see, they, unlike men and Jinn, don't belong to any one species. They are both and neither, and this can cause significant confusion. They are outsiders wherever they go. And being an outsider can be a terrible thing.'

'Yes, I know,' murmured Sharmeen, thinking of how traumatic it had been for her to transfer to a new school.

'Morpir was discovered by a practitioner of black magic. This man knew from his eyes what Morpir was, and he sought to tame his power for his own uses. So he taught Morpir all sorts of useless spells and gave him a home. Being a young Amluq, he didn't realize for a long time that he was being used by this sorcerer to procure things that no ordinary mortal could collect: screams, fears, doubts. As Morpir grew older, he began to realize that the dark magic practiced by the sorcerer was fake.'

'Fake? You mean black magic doesn't exist?'

'I mean that it is an illusion. The real power that humans have is in their minds. Think about it like this: If you concentrate hard enough, Sharmeen, you can move physical objects without touching them.'

'Telekinesis!' exclaimed Sharmeen.

'Yes. The fact is, humans are capable of miracles through their minds. But black magic teaches them the opposite: it casts a veil over their eyes; convinces people that they need other gods, other people in order to achieve their dreams. It teaches them to surrender their souls to Illusion. The creatures of dark magic are not magical, you are. But they usurp your powers, making you think you are useless. They are the parasites that need you to survive; they suck your blood, and in doing so forget that you have the power all along to cast them off. This is what the sorcerer did to Morpir for a long time. Until Morpir realized he had been free all along. He abandoned his master and took to wandering the world, discovering slowly that there is great power in being an outsider. He befriended shamans in Africa and lived among tribes that were said to have power over Jinn. They used dark magic to lure Qarin into temporary allegiance with them—to bring them things such as the corpses of newborns or the screams and curses of abused women. From this tribe, he collected these "gifts"—he knew that fighting evil required some cooperation with it. So he offered the sorcerer, who had me trapped, a vial of a scream; because he knew it would be useful for his dastardly tricks. Black magic needs hatred, pain, jealousy—the basest of emotions—to fuel it. The scream of a distressed child was too precious for the sorcerer to pass up. Thus Morpir bought me and set me free. He told me that my salvation lay in helping those who required my assistance. If I ever saved the life of a human, then the stain on my soul would be cleaned. I asked him to give me one such opportunity, and it was then that he asked me to respond to the caller of the silver prayer beads. And so here I am.'

Sharmeen remained quiet, staring at Jugnu as he rolled a few more clods of earth into a neat pile. 'Jugnu, do you think Aziz is practicing black magic?'

'What makes you ask?'

Sharmeen related her suspicions: the dead crow, Nani's warning, the manner of her death. Jugnu remained quiet as he climbed up the clods of earth. 'You may have a point. But before I can confirm anything, I will have to leave you for a while.'

'Where?' Sharmeen asked with alarm.

'Do not worry, I will not abandon you. But I must listen to the past and to the memories of this house. That will take up all of my energies, which have been focused on you.'

Sharmeen calmed down. 'Is that something else that Jinn do? Listen to memories?'

'Indeed. Did you know that sounds never die? They hang around in the air, upside down like bats, so soft that even a whisper seems a shout compared to them. Every word ever uttered lives forever in the space it was birthed. It has its own frequency. Your ears are not powerful enough to hear them, but your hearts are sensitive to their energy. That's why houses can feel happy or sad—because the words lodged in them are thus. If you sleep in a room where people have fought and cried, you will feel depressed and have nightmares. That's the way it is. I must listen to the words in your house to understand what has happened in the past. Your grandmother went too soon. She gave you glimpses, but not a complete story. I need to find out what or who killed her, whether Aziz is the villain that you say he is. But to listen to the voices, I need to gather my powers of concentration, which are at their best when I'm my invisible self. So while I do a bit of investigation, you need to protect yourself.'

'I will.' Sharmeen nodded solemnly.

'*If* Aziz is a practitioner of black magic, you must pray on the silver beads every day and keep them with you at all times. Be civil so that he doesn't suspect anything untoward. But stay away.'

A familiar feeling of gloom descended upon Sharmeen. To get Jugnu only to lose him seemed to take her back to her depressing life. She'd only known him for two days, but his presence invigorated her, like the fresh spring breeze. She knew she had to be strong, but she didn't feel like it yet.

'I understand, Jugnu. But please don't take too long.'

'I shall try not to.'

Sharmeen rose slowly and looked down, but the beetle was gone, leaving only clods of earth assembled in a neat pile. She slumped and walked back to the house to get ready for school.

Chapter 12

Aliya lay in bed, resenting the long fingers of the sun intruding upon her stupor, dimming the vibrant images of her memories that played out more clearly against the darkness. In her musings, she would see Amir alive and well once again, surprising her with his bear hugs when she least expected them. He'd caress her hair, his warm breath against her ear would make her shudder with anticipation. Now, he lay distant and still. She missed his arms, the indentations between the muscles and the tendons that were her bulwark against an uncertain world.

She rubbed her temples to massage the ache out of them, but her finger hurt: the shard of the glass bangle had caused an inflammation. She ignored it, her gaze fixed on the knob of the side table's drawer, which seemed utterly indifferent to her plight, not caring that she was dizzy from too much sleep; that her body felt old and rusty; that she had recently lost her mother and was probably about to lose her husband as well. No, it didn't care at all. It existed, lifeless and inanimate, attached to a plank of wood without a worry in the world. How Aliya envied it. A part of her wished that she could magically disappear without the world noticing. The urge to completely give up was so strong.

It hadn't always been this way. Just after Amir had slipped into his coma, Aliya had spent her days and nights tending to him. She had brushed his hair and stopped only when clumps came out in her hand. She had feigned cheerfulness and diligently kept him informed of all that went on at his work place, in the country, in the house, in her heart. She told him about Sharmeen and the fights between her mother and Aziz. She had massaged him and turned him over and had almost had a breakdown when she saw ulcerated bedsores on his back and legs, leering at her. The coma was eating into him as a maggot ate into an apple. She could not bear to see his pain.

Lately, sadness and listlessness were giving way to a throbbing, deeper darkness that haunted her in the form of nightmares. She'd had the dream again last night: Amir walking towards the precipice of a steep cliff while she yelled at him to come away, inevitably knowing as one does in dreams that he would fall off. The terror and anxiety of expectation crippled her. Every night her legs turned to lead when she needed them the most, struggling but unable to move as Amir disappeared off the edge. And every time she woke up with the realization that she was relieved he was gone. We are the architects of our dreams and Aliya knew that she was beginning to hope for an end—whatever it may be, it would be preferable to this endless waiting.

How did she get here, Aliya wondered sometimes, even as her mind drifted off to the university days when she'd first met Amir. How young he had been! And how handsome!

Aliya got up abruptly and shook away her thoughts. There was no point dwelling on the past when the present loomed so heavy upon her. But still, the memories came: Amir's visit to her parent's house; Amma had liked him and her father had instantly taken to him. He would make a good husband, they had said, because he was a Qazalbash, a warrior who would fight to protect what was his. And Amir was still fighting. But he fought alone, far away from Aliya.

Perhaps it was kinder to let him go.

But how does one decide to kill someone who is fighting to survive? To pry apart the fingers that still cling to life; to watch the love of one's life drift off because holding on is just too difficult. Just thinking about it sapped the energy out of her.

If only someone else could decide for her. Anyone else. Her mind whirled in desperation—and she thought of Aziz. Aziz. Such a solid name. She could lean on him forever and he would never buckle under her weight. Good old Aziz, with his starched kameezes smelling of cardamoms and Lipton tea-bags.

She walked down the corridor, hurrying through it to the kitchen, a tiny room with a rickety table in the middle, on which lay her breakfast tray. Her soft-boiled egg had not yet been peeled. Cracking the shell with a fork, she began to pry it away. Her finger smarted, so she held it up, trying her best to avoid contact, using her nails wherever she could. Little pieces of shell clung obdurately to the soft membrane underneath. She impatiently clawed at them and broke the egg. Gooey yoke fell on the floor, as if disembowelled. She slammed her fist on the table and cursed loudly.

'Bibi?'

Aliya leaned against the counter and looked back at Aziz, who was carrying vegetables in a polythene bag.

'I...I just wanted to peel this, but I spoiled it,' she explained petulantly.

Aziz put the bag down and took another egg out of the fridge. 'I can do it for you.'

'Thank you,' she said gratefully, raising her finger gingerly in the air to avoid contact with the metal of the fork that she held. Aziz saw the red, swollen tip and asked, 'Bibi has injured her hand?'

'Oh, it's nothing.'

'It doesn't look like nothing,' he said, peering at it with a strange intensity.

'Well, the day before Amma...before the ceiling fell, I was making Sharmeen's bed and found a broken bangle. One pricked my finger, that's all. It should have healed by now, though.'

Behind her, Aziz stiffened. 'I hope Sharmeen Bibi wasn't hurt?' he asked.

'No, I threw them away before she could find them. When Doctor Nawaz comes today, I'll show it to him. Meanwhile, I think I'm out of sleeping pills.'

'I think Bibi doesn't need more sleeping pills,' Aziz interrupted sharply.

Aliya looked up to see what was wrong, but he had his back to her. 'Shouldn't we let Doctor Nawaz decide that?'

'Perhaps,' he said, shrugging his shoulders, his white kameez clinging to his back, drenched in the heat of the afternoon.

Puzzled by his brusqueness, Aliya focused on the boiling water on the stove, watching her reflection in the shiny smooth bubbles; little concave mirrors that popped into oblivion.

***

Sharmeen drooped under the load of the schoolbag, the straps cutting into her shoulders as she walked back home from school. If she had friends, then she could have called and asked them over to play. But these days she found talking to people her own age tedious and exhausting. Nani had been her only confidante.

Washing her face and hands, she brooded over the sad fact that she wouldn't be meeting Jugnu for a while. Preparing to eat a lonely lunch, she walked into the dining room and cried out in delight.

'You're up, Amma!' she cried, giving Aliya a tight squeeze.

'Yes I am! I thought that I would stay up and have lunch with my baby; and then we can spend some time together after you're done with homework. What do you say?'

'I say that's amazing!' Sharmeen exclaimed, hugging her mother again.

'Uff, not so tight, you'll break my bones. Now sit down and eat. Aziz, can you bring Sharmeen some roti?'

He walked in, smiling. 'Of course. Freshly made. Nice and warm.'

Sharmeen was too happy to feel any guilt about her last encounter with Aziz. Ignoring him, she focused on her mum, chatting with her about her day as she ate. She anticipated a protest from Aziz, turning her away from her mother's side, but it never came.

In fact, the following days were the most peaceful since Nani died, as Sharmeen had unfettered access to her mother. Aziz generally kept to himself and smiled benignly at them from a distance—watchful but thankfully non-interfering. Her mother still slept a lot, and Sharmeen often roamed the house aimlessly, hoping for a firefly in the dark, or a dung beetle in her drawer, but things were definitely looking up.

Two months after Nani's death, they went to the graveyard where she was buried. Sharmeen stared numbly at the mound of earth covering her grandmother's remains and watched Aziz pour water to settle the dust. She sprinkled rose petals on the grave and lit sticks of incense and stood them in the mud. Was Nani even there? Sharmeen imagined her grandmother sleeping serenely underneath; her hands folded on her stomach, her white sari still neat and clean. Of course, scientifically, this was not possible—the decay would have set in. She had researched decomposition in school, the maggots would have eaten away most of the flesh. The intestines would be the last to go. The entire body would let out fumes and gases, which the earth would then absorb. It wasn't a pretty process. Standing above the ground, Sharmeen thought that all of this was still probably taking place below her feet. She was probably standing on her grandmother, which was not the most polite way to mourn her.

She looked at the foot of the mound. She tried to imagine her grandmother sitting there holding her arms out, waiting for a hug. Perhaps the dead were lonelier than the living? Perhaps they longed to be spoken to, to be remembered, to be touched, but the living just went on with their lives, forgetting because it was necessary? Sharmeen hugged the headstone and whispered softly, 'I haven't forgotten you, Nani.'

How many more stories had she lost when Nani died? It was an unbearable thought, and one that haunted her as she walked alone in the garden wondering where Jugnu was, whether he'd found anything out, whether the voices had whispered to him, unravelling the mysteries of the house.

One particularly humid evening, when the idea of walking was too taxing, Sharmeen crawled into Nani's bed, about to doze off when she was startled by a hiss, then a whisper, then a moan. She opened her eyes and felt as if she was falling, as if her mind hadn't been prepared for her body to wake up just yet. She saw herself float back down into her body, landing down with a rude jerk—watching her feet spasm upon contact. It was growing darker outside. Sharmeen groaned and put a pillow on her face, wanting its softness to sink into her.

'Psst...'

Sharmeen started, looking around frantically.

'Psst...' the sound came again, from the wall behind her.

Scooting to the foot of the bed, frightened out of her mind, she heard the voice again: 'Don't be scared. It's me.'

Her heart soared. 'Jugnu! Where are you?'

'In front of you.'

Sharmeen looked at the sheets, then the head of the bed, then the wall, which had the picture of a sunrise mounted on it.

'Where?'

A small creature slithered out from behind the frame. Her mouth curled up in disgust as she watched it move down and land on the headboard. It settled itself there and looked up at her with beady eyes, head cocked to one side, anticipating a reaction.

'A dung beetle and now a lizard,' she said, hugging her legs to increase the distance between them. 'Can't you turn into something *nice* for once, Jugnu? Why can't you become a firefly again?'

'Well, for your information, I am *not* a lizard, I am a gecko.'

'I see. *Why* are you a gecko?'

'Well, a firefly floating around the house isn't exactly inconspicuous, is it?' replied Jugnu, ambling down the board. Sharmeen drew her legs closer and felt slightly sick at the sight of the ugly brown thing on Nani's pristine sheets. 'A gecko, however, is our best disguise, especially when we're in spying mode. Generally humans don't want to have anything to do with us.'

'Yes, I'm certain that humans would leave geckos alone.'

'Mostly. Once, back in the days when I enjoyed causing mischief, I tried to scare a family of four sisters and one brother. It was such a promising proposition. I planned to startle them into disarray—the girls would run about and their brother wouldn't know whom to deal with, me or them. I figured it was a foolproof plan. So I made my grand appearance, falling from the ceiling right beside the youngest one's mattress. The boy screamed and ran out of the room and his sister whacked me with a sponge-slipper. The other grabbed a tennis racket and came at me, yelling "Die, die!" It was all so unexpected. Human women are very unpredictable, I tell you.'

Sharmeen giggled, but stopped as Jugnu came closer. 'Jugnu, could you stay there, please?'

The gecko stopped. 'Why? I want to see you better.'

'You know quite well why. I don't want to say anything, because the last time I commented on your disguise, you were offended.'

'So obsessed with appearances! Don't you know that you cannot fight evil unless you learn to understand that all is not as it seems?'

'I'll learn later,' Sharmeen insisted frantically.

'No. Learn now. Lift me onto your palm.'

'Jugnu, *no!*'

'Why are you so horrified? Geckos aren't that bad.'

'Could you change shape? Why don't you become a bird instead? A pigeon! There are a lot of pigeons on the roof. If someone walked in, I can say you somehow flew into the house.'

'*Pigeons?*' Jugnu sounded disgusted. 'Those rats on wings! Those carriers of disease! You would prefer a squawking, filthy bird over this sleek creature of subterfuge!'

'What do you have against pigeons?'

'Pigeons!' retorted Jugnu, spitting out the 'p' as if it disgusted him just to say the word, 'You do know that pigeons are the cursed ones, and they will signal the arrival of the Jinn with One Eye who will fight with the leaders of men to bring about total apocalypse. Mark my words, when the world will end and One Eye appears, it will be a pigeon that'll accompany him, pooping on his despicable shoulder.'

'But they are cute!'

'Cute? They fly all over the place and shoot their white faeces on your face, flapping their moulting wings when you want a quiet moment on the roof.'

Sharmeen giggled. 'Imagine a Jinn like you being afraid of pigeons.'

'Excuse me, I'm not *afraid* of pigeons, I merely don't like them, just as you don't seem to like geckos. There is no creature that can harm a Jinn, except a wolf, and thank goodness there are none in this territory.'

'Wolves can harm you?'

'Yes. They have an ancient power over Jinn. The wolf of a powerful Aalim was once beheaded by one of our kind; in return he laid a curse on our kind by giving the howl of the wolf a terrible power over us. We cannot transform in its presence, you see. If I am in the shape of a goat and a wolf comes along and starts baying at the moon, then

I'm not going to be able to fizzle into thin air. So I am mortal, bound by the body I'm in, which means I can be easily destroyed.'

'That's terrible. Is that why vampires and werewolves are always shown to be at war in all those storybooks?'

'Yes it is, but nice attempt to change the subject. Give me your arm.'

'Jugnu, I don't understand the point of this. I'd rather not.'

'I know you'd rather not, but you must learn to do things that are not pleasant if you want to be able to fight what your future holds.'

Sharmeen sat up straight and crossed her legs. 'What's happening? Did you find something out?'

'Let me climb on your palm and I'll tell you.'

Sharmeen sighed. 'You are as stubborn as a donkey, you know that?'

'Mule, you mean. And yes, I am. Now, your palm, please.'

Sharmeen closed her fingers and formed a fist. For a good two minutes, girl and gecko stared at each other in a battle of wills, but Jugnu was older, wiser and a Jinn, so Sharmeen knew she didn't really stand a chance. Relenting, she reached out and put her hand on the bed, wincing and cringing as the gecko crawled onto her palm. It was not slimy; in fact, it felt hard and dry. But the tail was another matter. It flapped about and tickled her palm.

'Jugnu, stay still. Else I'll drop you.'

'I'll send my tail after you!'

'Okay, you're on my hand. Now get off.'

'No. You have to look at me.'

'I don't want to.'

'Open your eyes, Sharmeen.'

She reluctantly obeyed, staring in horrified fascination at the gecko on her hand, brown like fresh dung, with a fat tail that rested on her wrist. It wasn't a terribly unpleasant face in fact, it was rather alert and intelligent.

'Well done. I'm proud of you. Now I want to climb your face.'

'*No!*' Sharmeen shrieked, horrified.

'Joking, joking. Now you see, this isn't so bad. You know, geckos were here long before you lot. They don't live in your house, you live in theirs. In fact, you must be very careful before trying to get rid of a gecko: you must warn it thrice before killing it, so that if it is, in fact, a Jinn in disguise, it can get away. People who start brandishing all sorts of tennis rackets and hockey sticks at us without prior warning are insensitive, not to mention silly: they're exposing themselves to danger, because a Jinn, even a good one, has every right to defend himself once threatened. And you don't want to upset a Jinn.'

Sharmeen imagined how ridiculous she would look if she warned a gecko to scoot before trying to kill it.

'But you don't feel ridiculous talking to a gecko right now, do you?' said Jugnu, hearing her thoughts.

'Well, I feel slightly ridiculous.'

'That's okay. You *are* slightly ridiculous. And always warn a gecko and give it time to get away. Don't do what Aftab Butt did.'

'Who was he?'

'Oh, he's the butt of Jinn jokes—pardon the pun. A very logical man: didn't believe in what he couldn't see or hear or feel. So one day, he saw a gecko sticking out of his drawer. Actually, it was the rump of a very fat gecko, its tail curling from right to left. He attacked the bedside table, and my friend would have been a goner if the gecko's tail hadn't fallen off. Lucky for him that he was able to get away—that would have been a pointless end to a good Jinn.'

'What do you mean?'

'If you kill a creature while the Jinn is still inside it, then you kill the Jinn. That's why assuming a human or animal shape makes us vulnerable, which is why it is recommended with great caution.'

'Jugnu, you should be careful...you shouldn't come to me like this...' said Sharmeen, growing alarmed.

'I'm flattered by your concern, little one. My choice of firefly and dung beetle is in line with the need for self-protection. Turning into a gecko is a bit dangerous, but only when it comes out of hiding. Anyhow, Butt Sahib tried to kill a Jinn and so he brought trouble upon himself. That Jinn took his revenge in the foulest way possible. He swooped up the drainage pipe and into the commode and the next time Aftab Butt squatted to, you know, excrete, the Jinn ate his way up into his bowels.'

'Jugnu, that's *disgusting*!'

'Isn't it? I would never venture into a man's bowels, no matter what the provocation. But my friend did and stayed there for a night and a day, making Aftab Butt howl in agony. They had to take him into the emergency room. They cut him open thinking that it was tapeworm, but of course, it was not. Poor Aftab never had a decent bowel movement after that!' The gecko chuckled and tittered and the movement tickled Sharmeen.

'Poor man. He didn't deserve such a harsh punishment, Jugnu. But I thought that Jinn couldn't easily possess grown men?'

'Oh, he wasn't possessing Aftab, he was inhabiting him. Possession means climbing inside and trying to exercise control. My friend just created indigestion and gas. A lot of it. That's why Aftab Butt's wife left him—she couldn't handle the smell.'

'That was very disloyal of her.'

'What did you expect? Women, in my opinion, are faithless.'

'We are not!'

'I'm entitled to my opinion.'

'Where did you get your opinion from? Have you ever been married?'

'Good heavens, no! No sane Jinn would ever take up with a Janeeree.'

'Why not?'

'Well, for one thing, Janeerees are just as strong, if not stronger, than Jinn. So they can push us around fairly easily. Besides, they prefer men to Jinn. They find them to be more...*obedient*. All a Janeeree has to do is knock a human male on the head to mesmerize him—he will be eternally hers, following her around, doing her bidding. It's a more convenient arrangement, as you may imagine.'

'Oh. That's dangerous.'

'Indeed. And Janeerees are lustful creatures—giving men a choice of sex or death. Most men prefer the former, you understand. But then they are eternally bound to the Janeeree; only when the Janeeree tires of them will they be released.'

'Nani used to say her cousin had been killed and a Janeeree had taken her place,' remembered Sharmeen, 'because she treated her husband very badly and yet the husband continued to be besotted with her.'

'Your Nani might be right. Most shrews are Janeerees in disguise. But it's easy to spot one in hiding. They're not experts in the art of camouflage like we are; sometimes they get transference all wrong, some glitch in their system. A Janeeree can transform into a beautiful woman, but for some reason, their legs are always disgustingly hairy. A woman who refuses to show you her calves is definitely a Janeeree in disguise.'

Sharmeen wanted to discuss this further, but more pressing matters needed her attention.

'Jugnu, have you found out something about what's going on here?'

'I have. Bits and pieces. It takes a bit of time. I'm still finding out about what has happened. However, I have come to warn you about Aziz. Stay away from him.'

'But he's leaving me alone and Amma's getting better.'

'There are traces of black magic in his room. I found a squeezed lemon and a knife with blood on it. And some broken bangles. You must make sure he does not touch you, or offer you any gift that might hurt you.'

'Broken bangles and lemons? What does it mean?'

'If there is anything he makes that finds its way to your blood, then he can influence you. This is the vilest of all spells, similar to the shenanigans of Qarins. It works like an insidious whisper, diffusing itself inside you until it has become a part of you without you even knowing it.'

Sharmeen grew more alarmed. 'But Aziz serves us food. I accept things from him all the time.'

'Recite the names of God every time you are about to eat. They are your best means of protection. What he is going to do, I cannot tell. His thoughts are garbled and I cannot hear them properly, which makes me suspicious.'

'But you can hear *my* thoughts. Why can't you hear Aziz's?'

'A Jinn cannot hear a person's thoughts for two reasons: either that person is a powerful Aalim and can block us; or he is himself under the influence of a Qarin.'

'You mean another Jinn?'

'Yes. You see, if a human is influenced by one Qarin, another Jinn cannot access his mind.'

'How do we know what the real reason is?'

'I'm not sure. But one thing is clear, he wants your cooperation and you must lull him into thinking that he has it. If he gives you a gift, which is the main way these people lure you into their enchantment, don't reject it. Take it, but dispose of it immediately. Pretend that you are softening to him. Let him open up to you; let him tell you his plans so that you can find out what I cannot.'

'Jugnu, tell me one thing. Is Aziz responsible for Nani's death?'

'It seems so, little one. But I cannot say for sure.'

'How?'

'I have visited the roof many times, little one. It is a spot of evil, where it seems all the joy and peace has been sucked into a vortex of despair. It reeks of black magic, the kind that kills: the sacrifice of one noble life to affect the death of another human, without physical intervention.'

Sharmeen remembered the final piece of the puzzle. 'The crow. Aziz killed it and mounted it in front of the house, on my hopscotch squares, to fend off the crows.'

'Not only did he kill it, he mutilated it—a life to take a life. Hatred, mutilation and one forceful wish to fuel the magic. That's all it takes to kill.'

'And Aziz hated Nani.'

'It seems he did. But can you blame him?'

'Are you defending the man who murdered my grandmother?' Sharmeen demanded flinging the gecko off her hand in anger. 'I don't care how Nani treated Aziz, she didn't deserve to die like that!'

The gecko sprang back to its feet. 'You must not judge, little one. Do not give way to hate in your heart; else you will be vulnerable to Aziz's antics. Black magic can only influence a mind that is weakened by hate, or fear, or both. Remember, all is not as it seems. Your Nani was not all good, just as Aziz may not be pure evil. The Jinn have been ordered to have faith in the human spirit, and so must you. To condemn is not your job, but that of the One Above.'

'He killed her...' cried Sharmeen, her eyes filling with tears as she remembered her grave. 'He killed her.'

'It is likely that he has caused her death, which is not the same as killing her. Only great pain and suffering can channel the volatile force of dark magic. He is a man in hell.'

'Good. He can stay there!' wept Sharmeen.

Jugnu ignored that. 'You must think of Aziz the scared little boy who did not receive kindness when he most needed it. That way, you will be able to stand him.'

Sharmeen buried her face in her hands and cried long and hard for her grandmother, for the injustice of losing her. Jugnu sat patiently, waiting for her grief to abate. When she wiped her face, she looked at the gecko and said, 'I'm sorry I threw you off my hand.'

'It is quite all right. In one moment of anger, you took advantage of your power, your size to hurt me, when I could have done the same to you. Aziz has been angry a long time and magic would give him power. Is he so unlike you?

Sharmeen bowed her head, feeling uncomfortable at the truth of Jugnu's words.

'It is not the exercise of power, but the control of it that is the true test of character. You must remember that.'

'I will, Jugnu.'

'Good. Now, I will take your leave.'

Sharmeen watched the gecko slither smoothly up the headboard, against which Nani used to rest her head. She started, a memory coming to her all at once.

'Jugnu, before she died, Nani mentioned that a pact had been breached.'

The gecko turned to face Sharmeen. 'A pact?'

'Yes. A pact that forbade the killing of a creature of nature.'

'Yes, the voices whisper about this pact; it comes through again and again when I listen. I shall have to disappear for a while again. Remember, gain Aziz's trust,' said Jugnu, crawling back up on the wall and disappearing behind the frame, 'but you have to remember to be brave.'

And in a moment, Sharmeen was alone in the dark, once again.

Chapter 13

Bad things come in three, Nani used to say. This evening, as Sharmeen walked with Aliya, her grandmother's words echoed in her mind as she counted: One—Abba's accident; Two—Nani's death.

A few days after Jugnu's last appearance, Aliya decided to have a conversation with Sharmeen. 'How's school? Have you made any friends?' she asked.

'Some.'

'And how are the teachers?'

'They're okay. I don't like my Math teacher though: she was born on October 31st. That's why every class is like Halloween.'

Aliya chuckled and squeezed Sharmeen's hand. 'My poor baby. Math has always been a struggle for you, hasn't it? Your father was very good at it, he would have helped you.'

'No need to worry. When Abba wakes up, I'll ask him.'

Aliya stopped walking and ran her hand through Sharmeen's unbraided hair.

'Beta, have you thought about what will happen when...
if...Abba doesn't wake up?'

'He will,' said Sharmeen stubbornly.

'You know, next week it will be seven months since
the accident. Amir's condition is worse. He's losing a lot
of weight. Chances are that his body will give way before
he wakes up.'

'He'll wake up soon, Amma.'

'Doctor Nawaz suggested that we should let him go,'
Aliya said softly.

'Let him go?'

'Yes.'

'What do you mean?'

'Sweetheart, the doctor has suggested that we should
stop giving him his food. He will grow weak and pass
quietly. It's the kindest thing to do.'

'You want to *kill* Abba?'

'Beta, try to understand. Even Aziz thinks...'

'Aziz! Who is he to decide what can be done with my
father?' screamed Sharmeen, pulling away as her mother
reached for her. 'I can't believe you would listen to *him*
of all people!'

'It's not an easy decision for me either. But we need
to think of Amir.'

'No, we're not thinking of him,' cried Sharmeen
vehemently, hugging herself and pulling away from her
mother. '*If* we were thinking of him, we'd be figuring out
how to wake him up instead of starving him to death! No,
don't touch me. I can't believe this. You're *such* a coward!'

Nani was right! You won't fight for *anything* because you're weak!'

'Sweet...'

'No!' Sharmeen covered her ears and ran away, sobbing as she crossed the lawn and corridor into Amir's room, banging the door shut. Minutes ticked by and she wept unabashedly, covering her face so that her hands were soaked wet with snot and tears. She wiped them on her jeans and sat down next to her father, desperately willing him to wake up.

'Don't let them kill you, Abba,' she said, 'Please wake up and show them you're alive. *Please* come back to me.'

She buried her head next to his arm and tried to calm down. She matched her breath with his: slowly, steadily, inhaling, exhaling, feeling a sense of connection with their communal breathing, as if they were somehow communicating. He was alive and he was hanging on. She looked at the small bump beneath his kameez: the tube from which the food was directly transferred to his stomach.

Aziz was feeding her father too. How could Abba protect himself from him? Sharmeen said a quick prayer, blew on her father's head as was the custom, and placed her hand in his palm. She felt his finger twitch against hers, ever so slightly. She looked at her small hand in his frail fingers and saw them twitch again. She stood up and leaned over Amir, peering at his face. 'Can you hear me? Wake up, Abba.'

But there was no more movement.

Her mind whirled with impatience and rage, most of

it directed at Aziz. What had he said to her a few days ago? That she was like a daughter to him? That he was her second father? Sharmeen pursed her lips and put her head in her arms.

She heard a loud knock on the door. 'Sharmeen Bibi! Why have you locked this door? Open it!'

She wanted to tell him to get lost. But she could not. She walked slowly to the door and slid the bolt. Aziz opened the door.

'Aliya Bibi is crying outside and I heard you slam the door shut. Is everything alright?'

'I'm okay. I just need to be alone with my father.'

'I understand. But don't lock the door. It worries me.'

'Okay,' said Sharmeen, feigning a smile. She watched him walk away. She needed to be clever, she realized. There was a problem to be solved here; it was confusing and scary, but it couldn't be solved without knowing what was going on. And the person who could tell her everything was Aziz. She'd have to talk to him, to find out his plans for her father. Then, she'd be in a position to do something about it.

The opportunity presented itself the next evening, when Aziz, squatting in the garden outside armed with a crescent-shaped sickle, was scooping out the weeds and tossing them onto a pile with an expert flick of the wrist. He was lost in his thoughts and looked up when he heard Sharmeen approach.

'Hello, Aziz.'

'Hello. What is my Bibi doing out alone? Where is Aliya Bibi?'

'She's inside, reading. I thought I'd come and see what you were doing.'

'I'm removing weeds and clearing the lawn,' said Aziz.

Sharmeen stood uncertainly, shuffling her feet. Nani, had she been alive, would have had a fit—to kill even the weeds would have been sacrilege. But since her death, flowers from the garden were being plucked and put into crystal vases all over the house. Pesticide had been administered to kill the ant colonies in the garden. No one else had died. She figured that punishment had been affected through Nani's death. So perhaps the rules were different now...perhaps, to gain Aziz's trust, she would have to be part of his world.

'Can I help you?' she asked.

Aziz beamed. 'Of course! Not with this though, it's too sharp. You take this khurpi here,' he said, giving her a hand hoe with a flat blade and blunt edges. 'Do you see these smaller weeds, these brown ones hidden in the grass? Now hold on to them firmly, no, not from the top, Bibi, you want to get them from the roots. There. Have you reached the base? Is there any further down you can go? No? Well, dig up the earth around, just like that, good, now, I want you to pull hard—oh ho—you didn't get the roots. You have to hold on very, very tight, here's another weed. Now, again, the base, yes, there you go, now pull! Well done!'

Sharmeen sat cross legged, combing the grass. 'Weeds are ugly,' she said conversationally.

'Oh, not ugly. They have their own beauty. But they don't belong in the grass. If you don't pull them out completely, they will grow back stronger and thicker. Pretty soon you'll have a forest of them.'

'Yes. Things that try to fit where they don't belong must be pulled out and chucked away.'

Aziz looked up suspiciously, but Sharmeen seemed engrossed finding more unwelcome intruders in the soft green. 'These weeds should be scared of you, Bibi. Pretty soon you will be their greatest enemy!'

Sharmeen kept her eyes on the grass. 'Shouldn't I be? After all, they are strong, they can grow anywhere they want. But they steal the land where all this beautiful grass is and kill it. If you ask me, weeds are cowards. They should find a place where they can stand tall and proud on their own.'

Aziz registered her words with silence. He put aside the sickle, deciding that enough work had been done for the day.

'In one way, Sharmeen Bibi, you might be right. But they don't grow here all by themselves. Their seeds are dropped here by the wind and the birds and the wasps and bees. They didn't ask to be put here. Fate brought them here. And they are strong, they need to survive. The strong must overcome the weak, that is the way of the world.'

Sharmeen dug the hoe in the ground and heard the soft tearing of tangled roots in the earth. 'I blame the grass for letting them live in the first place.'

'Or perhaps it is cruel for the grass to expect a living creature will stay in its place, not move and grow as all living things must. Weeds must have feelings too.'

Even though she hated him, Sharmeen could not help

but feel a pang of sadness for the small boy he'd once been, working hard, earning his keep and being scolded by a woman who refused to show him any kindness.

'Aziz, do you know anything about your family?'

Aziz paused. 'I have you. And your mother. You are my family.'

'And Abba too, of course.'

'Of course.'

'Were you there on their wedding day?'

'Yes, I was.'

'You and Abba were friends, right?'

'Oh yes. He called me his little brother. He made Aliya Bibi happy and for that I loved him.'

'I remember all of us used to play rummy on the weekends!' said Sharmeen, smiling.

'Yes. And he was always so proud when you made a proper sequence.'

'Yes,' chuckled Sharmeen, 'though I always forgot to count the cards. I won by fluke.'

'He was proud of you nonetheless,' smiled Aziz, picking up the sickle again.

'I miss him, you know. I can't wait for him to wake up.'

But Aziz remained silent, engrossed in the weeds. Sharmeen paused, not knowing how to continue. So she took the direct route. 'Amma said you think we should stop his food.'

Aziz didn't show any sign of surprise at this swift turn of topic. With great deliberation, he put the sickle down and squatted, resting his elbows on his knees. 'I think what the doctor thinks, Bibi.'

'Why does the doctor think we should kill Abba?'

'Not kill him. We should allow him to die.'

Sharmeen gritted her teeth. 'What if he wants to live?'

'Your Abba was my friend, Bibi. Above all things, I don't want him to suffer. Doctor Sahib says that if he does awaken, he will never be back to normal. He might not even remember who he is or who you are.'

Sharmeen sighed. 'What if I don't want to let him go?'

'Then I won't.'

'It is a decision that Amma and I have to make.'

'Your mother and I already agree with the Doctor Sahib,' said Aziz, his voice cold, his eyes on the ground. 'I think Sharmeen Bibi has to be brave, because she has to think about her father and not herself. And then she will realize that what her mother wants to do is out of love for her father. One has got to do difficult things for love, this is one of them.'

Her head spun with anger and frustration. Despite Jugnu's warning, Aziz's words struck a chord deep within her. She had never considered that her father might never be of sound mind and body again. She'd just imagined that he would one day open his eyes and hold out his arms with a big smile on his face and then all would be well. That he would wake up and yet not be himself was a devastating thought.

Sharmeen stood up, brushing the grass off her trousers.

'Aziz,' she asked, her voice composed. 'When does the doctor want to stop the feed?'

Aziz looked up at her, 'Whenever you and your mother are ready.'

'I need some time.'

Aziz held out his hand. 'Of course, Bibi. This is a difficult decision.'

Sharmeen didn't want to touch him, but she did so briefly. 'My birthday is in a week. I want Abba to be with me until then. After that, we will decide.'

'Of course.'

Aziz watched her walking away, her shoulders slumped and her head bowed. His heart went out to the little girl—it was a difficult time for her. He looked at the remaining weeds in the grass and decided to leave them be.

***

Sharmeen walked slowly towards the house with an ache in her head and a hollow in the pit of her stomach. How right Nani had been to suspect Aziz. Nani was a Watcher: She could judge people in one glance, pin them down like butterflies, and she was right to call Aziz a usurper, wanting to burrow his way into their family.

Sharmeen didn't want to be anywhere near him right now, so scooting behind the banyan tree, she sat down in order to be out of view from the house. Its shadow shed a dark halo on the grassless ground.

She sat cross-legged and uprooted clumps of dirt, throwing them in the air as angry thoughts swirled in her head like the beginnings of a tornado.

Closing her eyes, she tried to listen to the voices in the air, like Jugnu was probably doing. Waiting for answers was tiring. The air was cool, soothing. Exhaling again, she relaxed, crossing and uncrossing her legs, but froze when a clammy hand grabbed the back of her neck.

Jumping with fright, she looked around, but there was nothing except the banyan behind her. Its leaves rustled in the gentle breeze, hissing at her. She resisted the familiar fear that threatened to creep over her. Standing up, she pointed her finger towards the trunk, where an assortment of branches had twisted themselves together to make what looked like an old, wrinkled face, contorted with pain and agony. All her anger inside burst forth, channelled at those gnarled roots. Something malicious rose within her: a seething rage that would not be contained. It made her giddy with power.

'You can't have my family. You can try, but I'm going to stop you. You can't have anything. You don't belong here.'

For a moment, all was still. But then she felt a force suck all the power and bravado out of her, draining her hollow. And then Sharmeen heard it: a menacing, low-pitched laugh. *'You don't belong here'* it hooted, taunting her, throwing her words back at her. Sharmeen collapsed on the ground, feeling a chill crawl over her, biting and stinging its way up her spine. She looked up and saw an old woman in a black shroud, perched at an intersection of the branches, laughing at her, gesticulating madly, thrusting her fist in lewd gestures. Her cackle sent a shiver down Sharmeen's body, which was becoming more and more lethargic.

'You don't belong here,' the creature cackled, throwing Sharmeen's swagger back at her. She crawled on the branches with agile legs. The speed with which she moved belied her age—it didn't fit, it was terrifying. Sharmeen wanted to scream, but was paralyzed by the thick fear oozing over her, clogging her throat. Except she wasn't gagging, she was crying, watched by this sadistic creature who enjoyed watching her writhe. She wished she could faint to block out the fear, the demonic malice, the cackling that ricocheted around her.

She didn't know how long she lay there on the grass, under the shadow of the banyan, when strong arms swept her up. Sharmeen felt herself being carried away, but her eyes were fixated on the old woman who was still perched in the banyan. She heard a soft whisper, 'It will be all right, Bibi.'

In a daze, she allowed Aziz to carry her towards the house. She listened to his breathing as he murmured in her ear, 'Bibi must be careful not to sit under that tree. It is not a good tree.'

Sharmeen looked up at his face. His chin was squared and a vein popped in his forehead. He breathed heavily from the exertion of carrying her; which was funny, because she felt as light as a feather, floating in his arms, wafted into the house like the scent from a rose, laid on the sofa. As if from a distance, she heard her mother's voice, asking him what had happened. She felt her cool palm on her forehead.

'I found her sprawled under a tree. I don't know how long she was there. Probably half an hour or so. She was talking about Sahib. Perhaps her grief overwhelmed her.'

Sharmeen crinkled her brow in confusion. It wasn't the grief, it was the tree—hadn't Aziz just warned her against it? She was being hugged. She felt her mother's tear-stained cheek against hers. 'Don't worry, my love. We won't do anything to hurt you or Abba. We've got you, my jaan.' Sharmeen heard laughter. Hysterical, bubbling laughter. She looked up to see her mother's bewildered face above hers and Aziz's concerned face behind her mother's—two bobble heads swimming above her vision. She was out of breath—because the laughter that she heard was hers; and it came in waves, wracking her body with an intensity that made her chest hurt. She laughed for a long time, hiccupping, doubling over and burying her face into the sofa seat. And finally, after all the fear was spent and the hysteria had left her, she sank into a deep sleep.

Chapter 14

She was dreaming a pleasant dream. Someone was combing her hair—she smelt her father's cologne. She looked up and saw Abba, smiling and healthy, looking down at her with a twinkle in his eye. The fan whirred slowly above his head, making it look like he was wearing a giant helicopter cap.

'Don't leave me,' she whispered.

'I haven't gone anywhere.'

'Yes, you have. You're far, far away.'

'No. I'm with you. You just don't see me.'

'I do see you. I look at you all the time.'

'Then you need to *really* look. I'm waiting for you.'

Sighing, she closed her eyes. When she opened them again, it was not her father but the old woman with the demented grin leering at her, her pupils like empty black holes, sucking Sharmeen into their emptiness. She covered her eyes and sobbed in terror.

A strong pair of hands shook her furiously and she

awoke, bracing herself for another horrific vision but this time, Aziz leaned over her.

'Is Bibi having nightmares?' he asked gently.

'Aziz,' she whispered, 'what's happening?'

He did not give any outward sign of hearing her question. Sharmeen gladly drank the water he offered, relishing the cool wetness against her parched throat. 'You should rest. I'll stay here with you.'

'Answer my question.'

'Does Bibi not remember what Begum Sahib used to say? Never sit under a tree in the evening. Evil spirits will haunt you if you do.'

'You told Amma that I was sad about Abba. But you know it wasn't that.'

'I was just trying to calm your mother down.'

'So it's not just a tree?'

Aziz remained quiet. But Sharmeen pressed on. 'I saw a...a creature on its branches,' she confessed, desperate to share her burden.

Aziz started and paled. 'Creature?'

'Yes. It laughed at me. Made me feel so weak.'

'Don't think about her. She...'

'How do you know it's a woman?' she interrupted.

Aziz stammered and blinked. 'You said it was a woman.'

'No I didn't, *you* did. How did you know? Tell me!'

Aziz wiped his brow impatiently, glancing at the window to avoid Sharmeen's gaze. He stared at a spot on the wall above it, transfixed, the colour draining from his cheeks.

'Aziz? Are you okay?'

Sharmeen looked at the bare wall that he had focused his gaze on and a chill went down her spine. 'You see her too, don't you?'

Snapped out of his trance by Sharmeen's voice, he blinked at her, as if he had forgotten for a moment that she existed. 'I'm fine. Bibi must not worry about me, or about her father.' His lids dropped and he looked shifty.

'But the woman...'

'There's no woman, Bibi, just your imagination. Sometimes when we are stressed, we imagine things that are not there. You miss Begum Sahib. Therefore you see an old woman. But she does not exist.'

'She doesn't exist, just as the tree is not evil? Aziz, you're not telling the truth.'

He got up from his chair and drew the curtains so that the banyan could no longer be seen. 'Just forget about it. Now sleep. I will watch over you.'

He leaned back and closed his eyes, clearly not wanting to continue the discussion any further. It shouldn't have comforted her that he was there, but it did. And so Sharmeen drew up the covers around her and closed her eyes once again. This time, she dreamed of a swirling red rose in front of her, out of which a firefly emerged.

***

The next day, Jugnu returned. He crawled up to the bedstead and stared at Sharmeen who smiled weakly, letting him read her thoughts; too exhausted to express what she felt in words. Besides, the convenience of having a Jinn as a kindred spirit meant you didn't have to say anything at all—he'd understand perfectly.

It was difficult to see what Jugnu's response was, since all she could see was the vapid glance of the gecko. Its eyes were glassy—made more so by the periodic lick of a long tongue that diligently wiped them like a windscreen wiper. After a few minutes, she heard the deep timber of his voice.

'What a lot you've been through, little one. Do you know what any of it means?'

Sharmeen shook her head. 'Tell me what's happening, Jugnu.'

'I will. Better yet, I can show you. Do you trust me?'

Sharmeen nodded.

'Good. Close your eyes. Let your imagination do its work, let the images come.'

Sharmeen wrinkled her brow in confusion and Jugnu understood what she wanted to ask. 'When Jinn tell a story, we do so differently from human beings. Your grandmother relied on words: the rolling of her tongue formed sounds that created symbols in your mind. But there were too many gaps. Our stories, you can see, feel and touch. You are in them. We let you experience everything.'

Like muses in Greek mythology, Sharmeen thought to herself. She had read about them with her father—how they held writers and painters in a trance and gave them visions, the shadows of which they would later put on paper and canvas.

'Yes. All muses are Jinn, but not always benign. Some

want to show you a world to lock you inside it, so they can control your mind. For you to understand what happened in this house a long time ago, you must be present at the time when the pact was sealed. Then you will understand. Are you ready?'

Sharmeen nodded and closed her eyes. It was incredibly restful to be told what to do by someone she trusted implicitly. The darkness under her lids faded. A faint excitement stirred within her as she waited for the tale to be told. Faint echoes of lapping water played a gentle symphony in her ear, getting louder and louder until she was immersed in it. The story flowed over her like a gentle stream upon which she floated, buoyant as a cork. She *felt* the cool, radiant, sparkling wetness of the water; almost as if she was the water herself. How real this was! This world was so beautiful, she wanted to stay here forever. 'I wonder how poets wake up,' she wondered to herself.

Careful what you wish for. Jugnu's voice interrupted her. *The beginning of a story may be beautiful but it doesn't always remain that way.*

Sharmeen marvelled at the colours before her: verdant green grass, fiery orange gulmohar flowers hanging in bunches from deep brown branches. Above her, white clouds were suspended in the cobalt-blue sky, like wisps of chimney smoke. Sharmeen reached out and touched them, feeling their mist, wondering where they came from. A thrill went down her spine—she could go anywhere she pleased. One story would lead to another, revealing a world of endless possibilities.

Stay here, little one. Do not fly away with the clouds, you are needed on the ground. Do you see that man over there?

She looked in the direction of his voice and saw that the stream emptied into a murky brown lake. It lay beside a thicket of trees that stooped over it, their branches like mangled arms shielding it from the sky. On the bank knelt a frail man dressed in a voluminous robe.

Sharmeen walked over to him, his story seeping into her skin like warmth from the sun. This was her ancestor Aabid, an architect famed for the wondrous structures he had erected in Baghdad and Qum. People came from faraway lands to witness his mastery of design. Many wealthy sultans and wazirs begged him to construct their palaces, tempting him with riches, women, anything his heart desired. But Aabid was tired; no money could buy the peace that he craved.

His weariness washed over Sharmeen, pressing her down like lead. His wife, a raven-haired beauty with deep brown eyes had drawn her last breath with his unborn son still in her belly. He'd buried them under the shade of a century-old cedar and travelled to this land, where he wanted to build a new home by the water.

He wanted to start anew. But something lay beneath the murky depths of the lake by which he knelt. It sensed his intentions and did not take kindly to them.

Sharmeen felt a trickle of fear down her spine and she backed away, shivering. Just then, a firefly appeared before her eyes and led her towards the lake. She followed and stopped again by Aabid's side. Jugnu dove into the water, telling her to follow.

'I'll drown!' she protested.

It's a story. There is nowhere you cannot go. Come.

So Sharmeen obeyed. Her muscles clenched in anticipation of the cold water, but instead she found herself floating through a haze. There were creatures here that she couldn't see, but she could feel their restlessness.

Suddenly, she landed in a vast desert, under an unforgiving sun. Crescent-shaped sand dunes littered the surface and the wind howled in her ears, threatening a sandstorm. In the distance she saw a man, naked except for a tiny strip of loin cloth. His skin was burnt and his face was contorted. But he was running towards an island of green just beyond the tallest dune.

That is my friend. The one who left me behind to stay with the man we both killed.

He had become a foul, ghoulish creature who tormented travellers with visions of water that didn't exist, driving them to madness. This was what had become of Jugnu's friend who had fled the museum after killing the man, leaving Jugnu to face the consequences of their mutual villainy alone. She saw glimpses of the evil that had subsequently become habit for him: false whispers in husbands' ears about their wives' infidelity. She heard his laughter when innocent virgins were tortured and murdered. He had hacked off the limbs of babes and then sold the maimed innocents to earn money born of lazy pity. An unquenchable lust for mischief that had begun as soon as he had committed his first crime. He became uglier with each foul deed and Sharmeen saw him run towards the oasis, a burnt skeletal dwarf hobbling towards relief. Water beckoned him like fate.

The oasis offered relief from the burning heat and baking sand through cool shade and water. This bald, decrepit creature crawled into a small pond and thrashed about, laughing as if deranged. Drinking his fill, he cupped the water in his hands and poured it over his face. His body gleamed in the dappled shade of the palm trees. The more he drank, the larger he grew, taller and muscular. Sharmeen felt a powerful tug and dug her heels into the sand, refusing to be pulled. She felt his relief mixed with hatred and a terrible anger, the kind that fuelled tornadoes and floods. A voice, as old as Time itself, spoke and silenced his revelry: 'Thou hast drunk thy fill. Honour me, for I have given thee a new life. Bow down to Me and implant My Seed in the Upstarts. Dwell forever in the water—thy Eternal Abode. Water will sustain thee—from it thou are born and to it thou shalt return. Whisper to Man and his kind; drive them mad with thy craft. Emerge now as Sargosh the Whisperer and do thy Worst!'

The Jinn knelt in the water, his hand on his heart, pledging obedience. With one powerful surge, he stood up and looked around, his muscular body tense, needing fulfilment. Sharmeen felt his tumultuous energy; it emanated from him in waves. And then Sargosh smelt a woman, the wife of an old shepherd who lounged in her caravan, sweating and cross, dreaming of a lover. She drank from a tankard; red wine jostled and splashed against her lips as the caravan moved over uneven terrain. 'Enter her through the wine.' Sargosh's eyes gleamed, and he disappeared from Sharmeen's vision, his eyes the last to fade into thin air.

Jugnu appeared again and dove into the waters of the oasis. Sharmeen followed suit and found herself back in the murky depths near Aabid who still knelt in despair. But here too, Sharmeen felt the same restless energy; she knew that this was where Sargosh was: a water dweller, occupying this watery world to spread mischief.

This lake had become his kingdom, where he wreaked havoc upon any traveller who had the misfortune of straying. Several men bathed here only to howl in agony when something gnawed and sliced the skin off their legs. Word spread that the territory was haunted. Sargosh wasn't taking kindly to Aabid's plans. No, he was in an uproar at the audacity of this usurper, who must be driven away, tormented into madness so that he never dared to stray here again.

He hurled abuses at Aabid, reminding him of the pained cries of his wife as her insides were torn asunder because of the babe that he put inside her. Sharmeen listened with horror to the insidiously whispered accusations. 'You killed her with your lust, greedy man, just as you killed your son. Why do you come here, to our land? Do you think we will let you be in peace? Go kill yourself and join your scrumptious wife: put more of your seed inside her, tear her up once more. That is all you are good for. Selfish fool of a mortal, butcherer of wombs, twaddling here for a new beginning. Usurper. Fiend, worthy of nothing but Death...'

On and on he went until Sharmeen wept with the despair of it all, just like Aabid, who crouched on the ground, digging his fists into his ears to keep the voice out. But wherever he turned, his wife's lifeless eyes stared back at him accusingly.

Be careful, Sharmeen. People have lost themselves in stories like these. Stay focused. Something is about to happen.

The shade shifted. The sun climbed higher, its rays bathing Aabid, cleansing the dark halo of memories that Sargosh so expertly wove around him. His whisperings faded away. Aabid opened his eyes and wiped his face, staring at the light before him, dazed. Another sound caressed his ears: Sharmeen heard it too, the melodious cadence of a woman's voice.

'Aabid,' it called out, gentle as a lullaby.

He turned towards the sound. 'Aabid, build your house. The Jinn of this land give you permission. I will rid them and you of this Qarin.'

A golden glow began to spread over the land, until every blade of grass, every leaf and every flower was shining in a soft hue.

This is the shadow of a Janeeree, little one. One made from smokeless fire, living under the yoke of Sargosh and his whisperings, watching his tyranny over mortal men.

The Janeeree appeared as a woman, tall and statuesque, draped in a golden sari. She placed a hand over Aabid's brow. Her hand was slender, its veins prominent under her pale skin.

'Fill this lake with sand and earth. Build your house

over it, my weary traveller. I will protect you from this Qarin who would make a desolate graveyard of this verdant garden. This land belongs to us and we will share it with you, but on one condition. You must promise that your kin will protect our abode. No tree shall be uprooted, no flower torn from its stem, nothing will be cut down or demolished, for these belong to my kind; and we have lived here for many years. Any destruction will rejuvenate him that whispers to you and restore his power. We will then not be able to protect you against his mischief. Do you understand?'

'Why do you help me, a soul who's lost and damned?'

The woman smiled. 'To atone for a man I destroyed once, a long, long time ago.'

For a moment, the Janeeree seemed to look at Sharmeen, her blue eyes like mirrors reflecting the face of a weary traveller in thrall of a demon he had impregnated. In that instant, Sharmeen knew that this was the Janeeree of Nani's stories, the oldest of the land, and this was her penance for the life she had destroyed. Her willow had been chopped and a river of tarmac placed in its stead. She had floated on many a cloud and tarried in many a graveyard before coming to rest here, but Sargosh's tyranny reminded her of the many souls she had tormented. When she saw Aabid, she remembered the father of her lost son and his grief became her own. So now she offered him a truce, the first between Jinn and men, for only an alliance could protect both against Sargosh.

Aabid put his hand in hers. 'I will protect your land. I promise.'

The Janeeree smiled and kissed him on his forehead. 'Go. Find a new wife to warm your bed. She will give you daughters, many daughters. They will be the Watchers; we will show them signs so that they will know of our presence and we will gift them with silver. Remember, Aabid, if the pact is broken, devastation will come upon those who fail to guard this place.'

Sargosh flailed about as if trapped within the lake, making the land shake with his rage. Sharmeen was caught in what she realized was a massive earthquake. The waters of the lake churned and Sargosh emerged in a mist of black, dark like coal, bearing upon the Janeeree.

But the Janeeree had given her word. The only power to undo the work of Satan was love and sacrifice: the surrender of one for the sake of many.

As she faced her enemy, the Janeeree slowly changed shape. Her arms extended from their sockets to reach the ground, four more legs grew from her sides and the beautiful woman gave way to a fearsome creature. She snarled, but Sargosh towered over her. They fought a fierce battle. Sky-rending screams shook the land. Sargosh surged inside—drowning her. Sharmeen wept as she saw her crumple to the ground, assuming the shape of a woman. She submitted to Sargosh, opening her arms and legs like a flower yielding its scent. Black liquid oozed out of her nostrils and flowed to her legs, seeping inside the cavity in between. It was this invasion that the Janeeree awaited. Her limbs grew wooden around him, transforming into branches that fused around, encaging him inside. Her hair turned into orange flowers of flame and the black of Sargosh disappeared in the trunk of a stunted gulmohar. For a moment, it was as if she had prevailed, small leaves and flowers bloomed and the tree looked alive. Seconds passed, then minutes and there was a sickening crack. Black saplings emerged from the trunk of the gulmohar, crawling down to meet the ground. The creepers of the banyan began to take over and smother the gulmohar. The flowers wilted and drooped. Mahogany roots encircled the trunk-like thick ropes, until all Sharmeen could see was a twisted banyan, smothering and living off the gulmohar. The Janeeree offered her body to Sargosh knowing it would be hard for him to resist such a potent life source—he could survive on her for years without needing additional sustenance.

What made her do such a thing? Sharmeen wondered.

A desire to repent. With this sacrifice, she protected both Jinn and men.

How could a creature change so much? Perhaps all those years of guilt? Perhaps she was tired of suffering for her mistake? There were so many stories here, in this land that she had considered ordinary, isolated. She wanted to know them all. But now was not the time. She saw what Jugnu meant when he said it was easy to get lost in this world. It was like opening one babushka doll only to find another and then another, in endless continuity.

Sharmeen looked warily at the banyan: it was smaller than the one that existed now. She wrapped her hands around one branch and closed her eyes. She felt again the restlessness, heard the laugh.

So, Sargosh is still there?

No, little one. My old friend soon found another body to ravish, after he had consumed the last vestige of the Janeeree's life force. Needing more sweat, tears and blood, he needed another host to sustain him: and it arrived just in time. Look there.

Sharmeen looked around to see her house, standing tall and proud, the banyan tree looming over it and she saw a white ambulance pull up. She saw herself, holding her mother's hand, standing at the doorway with Nani. Dear white-haired Nani, looking small but formidable, descendent of Aabid and protector of his legacy. Out came Aziz, helping three other men carry the stretcher on which her father lay unconscious.

And just like that, she knew what was going to happen. She couldn't bear to watch. 'No, Jugnu! No more!'

You must know this, Sharmeen.

Sharmeen tried to close her eyes, which was difficult, for they were already closed. She saw tendrils of black smoke extending from its gnarled roots, sharp and pointed like fingers. They crept their way across the garden. Sharmeen could feel the lethargy creep over her.

Resist, little one.

Sharmeen shook her head and looked up again, to see the wispy curls enter her father through his nostrils, disappearing in his frail form.

'OUT!' she screamed. 'NO MORE! I can't do this! Get me out!'

And Jugnu relented, wheeling her back into her room.

The dizzying effect of the return fazed her. The world spun round and Sharmeen felt queasy. But the revolutions dropped pace and soon she found herself breathing to the slow rotation of the fan above her. She looked around, but there was no gecko, no firefly. She was alone. The memory of the darkness that had sought refuge in her father's body rendered her powerless now.

'Sweetheart, don't put the blanket on your head,' Aliya's voice interrupted her reverie. 'You might want to breathe in the fresh air. It will make you feel better.'

Her mother's voice sounded unfamiliar after all the horror she had witnessed. Sharmeen felt a hot, liquid wave of resentment. People like her mother were lucky. Weak, but lucky because they had no sense of how many invisible dangers engulfed them at every waking moment. No wonder Nani had resented Aliya. Protection was a tiresome business.

She was the protector now, she realized. Nani had passed the responsibility onto her. She needed to save her father from Sargosh, do something, anything, to get him out so that her father could return to them. She needed to think and her mother's concerned face wasn't helping her concentrate.

'Amma, I want to be alone,' she said curtly, her tone not unlike her grandmother's. Aliya stiffened, but Sharmeen was tired. She sighed with relief and covered her head with the blanket once again as her mother closed the door behind her.

Chapter 15

Night lent its black shade to the grey evening. As the house of the gulmohars descended into darkness, a tall figure rushed out into the street, into the sudden sandstorm that offered respite from the heat. A black chaadar obscured his face. His eyes burned as the sand found its way to the back of his throat, choking him, yet he hurried on. His mission was urgent.

Baba Baqsh's hovel stood behind the graveyard, next to the old vegetable bazaar. It was flimsy, its roof nothing more than five large pieces of corrugated tin held together by some rope, propped up by bricks. Aziz entered the shack, pulling aside a dirty grey curtain crawling with dust mites.

An old man lounged on a tattered red and blue cloth on the ground. His beard—long, curly and tangled with grains of rice and a yellow, creamy substance congealed within—overwhelmed his face. Only his lips—fleshy and drooping—showed through his wiry whiskers. With his hooded gaze and vacuous expression, he seemed to be in a perpetually drugged stupor.

An emaciated boy pressed his legs diligently, not even bothering to look up at their visitor. A few black-coloured candles flickered depressingly to cast a low light on Baba's green caftan that had been mended several times with colourful patches of orange and yellow. In the corner was a small mattress, the thickness of a blanket. A hookah lay next to it and the smell of hashish wafted from it—Baba's nocturnal entertainment.

The smell of chicken and goat droppings coupled with the faqir's own stench made Aziz sick to the stomach. But he had no choice; he sat cross-legged and offered a wad of hundred rupee notes, the ritual donation for services rendered.

Baba Baqsh waved his hand and the boy scrambled up to scoop the money, depositing it in a rusted tin box under the candles. The faqir was famous in these parts, known to spend his days posing as a beggar and his nights collecting bones from the graveyard to create talismans and spells to sell to anyone who wished to change the course of their lives.

He reclined on his green chaadar filled with brown, sticky stains, picking his nose philosophically as Aziz squirmed before him. It was a rule that you didn't speak to Baba before he spoke to you.

'Tell me, my son,' he said finally, 'did my bangles achieve the desired effect?'

Aziz bowed his head. 'No, Baba.'

The faqir sat upright, suddenly alert. 'Did you put them on the young girl's bed, like I told you to?'

Aziz nodded vigorously. 'I did, but her mother got to them first. She threw them away.'

The faqir leered. 'Oh, is that so? She must be eating out of the palm of your hand then? Listening to everything you say? Tell me, does she cling to you like a vine on a wooden branch?'

Aziz curled his lips in disgust at the Baba's crooked, rotten teeth revealed by his grin. Sexual conquest was not what he looked for. 'The mother was never a problem. But the girl resists me. Your prayers do not work because they haven't seeped in her blood. She has not been pricked.'

'Did you draw your blood and mingle it with lemon in her food?' Baba enquired, as if discussing a housewife's recipe.

'I did, but to no avail. She does not trust me and she must, otherwise it will be difficult for me to protect her. And I am running out of time.'

'Out of time, you say?

'Yes. Sharmeen sees the woman too.'

'The woman? The one in your visions?'

Aziz nodded. Although he didn't admit to Sharmeen, he knew the creature well. She was a fearsome sight: a small woman, the size of a bat, lounging about in places he least expected, her presence like a black, thick cloak covering his mouth, preventing him from screaming at the sight of her blood-shot, leering eyes. When she opened her mouth, a sharp yellow tooth protruded from her gum, and from behind that tapered a thick, wet tongue that slid out like a fat snake and licked her chapped lips as she jabbed at him with bony fingers. He felt her presence all the time. When he closed his eyes, he heard her cackle and when he covered his ears, he felt clammy hands smother his face. The woman could come any time, when he least expected her.

And then the nightmares came. Of Aliya being hung and disembowelled—of Sharmeen being dragged across jagged stones by her braid, her blood crimson on the grey ground. And every dream ended with a dead crow, mutilated, plastered on the spike.

Baba Baqsh had listened carefully to Aziz's complaints and provided several talismans, but still the nightmares had persisted. Then one day Aziz woke to a whisper: *Kill*, it had said, *Impale. Pluck the flowers. Destroy.* At first he resisted, knowing it was against Begum Sahib's rules. But the voice was relentless and he had to obey just so it would leave him alone. The last thing he had expected was Begum Sahib's response—or her death. Her violent, gruesome death—caused by him and him alone.

He shifted uncomfortably. He was the cause but it was not his fault. No. He could not have known. He ran to Baba Baqsh and cried to him, protesting his innocence. The faqir had merely smiled, not believing him. Innocence was determined by intentions. Maybe the woman was a figment of his imagination—a symbol of his subconscious who wanted to avenge all the hurt and pain Begum Sahib had caused.

The suggestion had filled Aziz with despair. On the one hand, it was his duty to serve the wife of the man who took him off the streets, taught him to read and treated him like a son. But it was Begum Sahib who relegated him to the servant's quarters after her husband's death, isolating him from Aliya.

But this was no time to nurse his guilt. Returning to the present, Aziz pressed on with the matter at hand. 'She is not just in my head, Baba. The creature made itself known to Sharmeen. The girl fainted with fear.'

'That means she is real. The evil is growing in your house,' Baba Baqsh claimed, rolling his eyes and muttering as if to find a cure for the predicament. Aziz watched him, waiting anxiously.

'Where do you see her most often, my son?' he asked finally.

Aziz thought about it. 'Though she appears all over the house, I feel her most next to Amir Sahib.' He closed his eyes, remembering the sensation of her in Amir's room: as if she was swooping inside, clenching Aziz's heart, squeezing until he thought he would die of pain.

Baba Baqsh arose from his stupor. His voice was different as he spoke: deeper, thicker. 'She lives in him. Smother him now—kill him before she finds another body to inhabit. If he dies swiftly, so does she.'

The thought hit Aziz like a tornado. His first instinct was to balk. He had wanted to let Amir go gently. To allow death was kindness, not murder. But what Baba Baqsh was suggesting—it was unjustifiable.

Baba Baqsh smiled. 'Why do you rebel against it? Remove one obstacle and solve all your problems. Isn't that the way of it?'

'I do not understand what you mean,' stammered Aziz, his gaze on the ground.

'Come, come. It is not in vain that I have passed the years to reach my advanced age,' Baba smiled. 'I see your eyes when you mention the mother. You long for her. Remove the husband and you can take his place.'

Aziz shook his head and got up, giving Baba a curt salaam. The faqir's taunting laugh followed him out of the shack.

Baba was wrong. Aziz loved Aliya, but not like that. She was like a sister to him. Had he hated Begum Sahib for putting an end to their closeness? Yes he had, he couldn't deceive himself on that front. But he hadn't killed her. And what of Amir? Amir was a good man and he made Aliya happy. He treated Aziz like a little brother and Aziz, always hungry for affection, had always received his love and regard with undying gratitude.

However, even if Baba was wrong about Aziz's intentions, his reading of the situation seemed correct. Amir suffered; and the creature, if it lived in him, bode grave ill, not only to Aziz, but to Sharmeen and Aliya too. If harsh measures had to be taken to protect them, then Aziz would not hesitate.

It made sense. The creature was just an image to him elsewhere, but in that room, she was real, a powerful spirit that seemed to drive a stake into his very soul, impaling him like he had impaled the crow.

It was dark when he reached the house. The storm had abated; Aliya and Sharmeen were fast asleep. If he had to act, now was the perfect time. To delay would be to invite more calamity. What if the creature reached Aliya? She would never be able to withstand such trauma. No. It was up to him to protect the family.

Aziz picked up a leather cushion—the gentlest way to kill Amir would be to smother him. He clutched it with both hands. He would end things now, when no one knew what he was up to.

The woman appeared again, hovering over him like a dark cloud. *Stupid fool! Turn back! Is this how you repay me after all my help? I got rid of the old hag for you. All for you—wretched vagabond, unworthy of love.*

As Aziz neared the room where Amir lay, it shrieked, its pitch cutting into Aziz's eardrums like shards of glass. He covered his head, which seemed to splinter into a thousand pieces. But still he persevered. He moved forward, feeling a slowly building sense of liberation; he was going to be free. Killing Amir would solve everything.

He walked slowly, one step after another. Steeling himself for the onslaught that was sure to come, he opened the door where the patient lay. And froze.

Amir's comatose body was wracked with violent convulsions, frothing at the mouth. He was having a seizure.

Chapter 16

Aliya watched Doctor Nawaz examine Amir's weak body. It was hard for her to believe that just an hour ago it had jerked with spasms. The shock of seeing her husband move had turned into horror upon the realization that it was due to agonizing pain. The seizure abated quickly and only when she felt the faint rhythm of his pulse did she sit and have a good cry.

The doctor took off his spectacles and rubbed the bridge of his nose. 'A strong man would not have been able to withstand an attack of this intensity, yet Amir has done so. It's a marvel that he survived. Aliya beta, have you considered my previous advice?'

'We discussed it, but Sharmeen isn't ready.'

'You both have a very difficult choice to make. Amir is disintegrating as we speak. The kindest thing to do would be to stop his sustenance; to unhook the oxygen so that he goes, as nature meant him to. The possibility of him ever waking up is slim...'

'Slim? Or impossible?'

Doctor Nawaz pursed his lips, his brown eyes looking at Aliya's frail form with sympathy. 'Nothing is impossible, beti. But the decision is yours to make.'

She wiped her eyes with the palm of her hand.

'Your little girl wants to hold on to her father. That's understandable and she's been through a lot herself. But children are resilient, that is all I can say. I have given you my opinion, but ultimately, I will respect what you decide.'

Aliya looked at her comatose husband struggling for breath. He was not going to wake up. She knew this now. She got up, walked to her husband and kissed his forehead. And then she felt it—a power draining her, sucking the life out of her.

Doctor Nawaz, quick on his feet for a man of his age, caught her before she hit the ground.

***

Things were falling apart, Sharmeen thought later as she recalled the events of the night. Doctor Nawaz had prescribed a sedative for Aliya on Aziz's insistence. That morning, Aliya had sat her down and talked to her about taking the doctor's advice. Abba was dying, and it had been decided that he would be helped along in the process. Sharmeen would have created a fuss, but her stomach was cramping terribly and her back hurt and her legs felt like lead. She knew she needed to save her father, but with the onslaught of nausea, she realized she needed to save herself first. What a ghastly last day of her twelfth year!

She lay in bed, watching the banyan tree—no longer secret, no longer mysterious, but just as evil. She stared at its branches, tap-tap-tapping at her window, feeling increasingly uncomfortable. Perhaps she was being possessed? No, possession wouldn't entail going to the bathroom every five minutes. Or did it? She'd been feeling like this for a couple of hours. Possession was probably a faster affair.

She got up to visit the toilet one more time and froze as she saw a red patch on the bedsheet. What was this? Another illusion? No. She felt a warm viscous substance on her thighs and immediately knew that this was what Nani had told her about, referring to it clinically as menses.

Sharmeen wondered whether to tell her mother about it—she would have dearly loved some advice. But Aliya was asleep, so she went to the closet, took a sanitary napkin and fresh clothes and disappeared into the toilet. When she came out, she was composed and focused on scrubbing the stain off the bedsheet.

She felt Jugnu before she saw him, the scent of mountain breeze accompanying him. He was here.

'Where are you?' she spoke out loud.

'I'm here, little one. You can sense me?'

'Yes I can. I...um...really need my privacy right now, Jugnu. Could you come later?'

'I will do just that. You have bled?'

Sharmeen blushed and looked accusingly at the bed, as if it had unwittingly let out a forbidden secret. 'I really don't see why you have to be so direct about it...'

'Yes or no. There's no time for shyness.'

'Yes. Now go away.'

'I will, but I've come to warn you: stay far away from your father's room. Don't let Sargosh get a whiff of you.'

'Doesn't a Jinn's sense of smell diminish with possession, like his power?' she asked irritably, going back to scrubbing the sheet furiously.

'It does indeed. This is the only reason you are safe for now. Other Jinn can smell you from a mile away.'

'Jugnu, you're embarrassing me.'

'I do apologize, but I must be blunt. Our kind have a special sense of this stuff.'

'Listen, I do *not* want to discuss this.'

'But it has relevance: do you think it's comfortable for me? If you could see me, I am squirming with embarrassment. Wriggling like a worm. Writhing in agony...'

'I get the picture.' Satisfied that the stain could no longer be seen, Sharmeen proceeded to the bathroom, where a gecko slithered across the mirror. 'Jugnu could you JUST give me some privacy!'

'I AM!' came the irritated voice from outside.

Sharmeen turned to look outside and jerked her head back to look at the gecko, which had frozen in fear the minute she had yelled, as geckos are wont to do when they are not Jinn. 'Sorry,' she apologized to it as she washed the towel and hung it to dry.

She went back and lay down on her stomach, putting a pillow under her thighs to give her back some ease. 'Jugnu, I'm in pain.'

'Poor little one. I really don't know what you're going through; therefore I can give no advice.'

Sharmeen smiled. The discomfort was apparent in Jugnu's voice. 'Could you take some shape, Jugnu? It's a bit odd speaking to no one in particular.'

'Why? Most people do it all the time.'

'Please?' she pleaded.

'Well, alright. Here I am.'

Sharmeen saw a firefly emerge out of thin air. It looked like a house fly because it didn't glow in the day time.

'Did you hear what Amma has decided about my father?'

'I did.'

'They've probably already discontinued the medicines.'

'No they haven't, little one. They will stop once your birthday has passed. I heard your mother tell Aziz so.'

'My birthday's tomorrow. Jugnu, what are we to do?'

Jugnu perched upon her hand.

'Your father will not die. Sargosh will not let him. He needs a body to prey on. But he will look for a new host when he gets the chance, which is why you are in grave danger. You are no longer a child and the scent of you will tempt him to no end.'

'Why doesn't he go for my mum?' asked Sharmeen irritably, and then checked herself. 'I mean...I'm glad that he hasn't, but he likes women and Amma would be easy.'

'Remember the story, Sharmeen? Sargosh was weak at the time he changed hosts: your father put up no resistance. An adult human female will be a tough task and he dare not risk it. He needs to feed off your father before he grows strong enough to switch bodies.'

Sharmeen shuddered at Jugnu's clinical terminology. 'And now?'

'Do not go near Sargosh or your father. You will be possessed.'

A sudden thought startled Sharmeen. 'Jugnu, Abba's seizure yesterday—was it caused by Sargosh?'

'As you know, I do not have access to whomever Sargosh possesses. But it would be my guess that Sargosh would not jeopardize the body that sustains him. No, I would imagine that your father is weakening, but Sargosh is keeping him alive.'

'Then we can't let him slip out of Abba!' exclaimed Sharmeen.

'I know. Ironic, is it not? He who has caused so much death is now responsible for your father's life.'

'But if Sargosh is possessing Abba, then who is the woman? Is she another spirit?'

'No, she is a trick of his creation. You see, when a Qarin possesses a full-blooded human, all his energy is used up in influencing his thoughts and decisions. But Sargosh's powers are not as depleted by inhabiting your father's frail body. As a Qarin of Iblees, his job is to do his best to lead people astray. He is strong enough to project his memories on other people. And the old woman is a memory presented to scare all who can see her. Every Qarin has an emblem he chooses to scare people with. This woman is his.'

'Why her?'

'The old crone that you see actually existed. Back in the day when Sargosh and I were young, we used to visit a village to have fun and play pranks on the people there. This woman was the local town beggar, homeless and wretched. I still remember the way she sat next to a gutter and wet a week-old chapati with her spittle so it was soft enough to gnaw at. She was a pathetic sight with hair full of lice and a gummy grin. A yellow tooth moved when she pushed it with her tongue. She was all alone in the world and her isolation made her mad. She was paranoid that someone was practicing dark magic on her. She fascinated Sargosh; he always had a sense of the macabre.'

'She sounds tragic.'

'Yes. It's appropriate, isn't it? A figure of sadness to spread more grief.'

'Aziz sees her too, Jugnu. He won't admit it though.'

The firefly buzzed a thoughtful circle in the air. 'This is not good. It means Sargosh is gaining power.'

'There's one more thing,' Sharmeen interjected, 'If he is growing stronger, can he not sense your presence?'

'Sargosh will be on the lookout for more bodies once your father's energies are depleted. He will be unable to detect my presence unless I want him to. Since the voices told me about him, I have kept my distance.'

'Then what's the solution, Jugnu? Amma will stop the feed, so Sargosh will need a new body. If he leaves Abba, Abba will die. I can't go near him. You can't go near him. Amma shouldn't go near him. Aziz will probably kill Abba if the lack of food doesn't. *What do we do?*'

'I'm not sure.'

Sharmeen hadn't expected Jugnu to say that. Jugnu

was the solution to everything. He could see the unseen, he could listen, and he was the finder of secrets. That he didn't know how to proceed frightened her deeply.

Jugnu sensed her alarm. 'It is time you and I got some help. We must go to someone older and wiser than us.'

'Who?'

'Morpir.'

Sharmeen felt a chill take over her limbs. 'He...he's here?'

'No, we will go to him. He will know what to do.'

Jugnu did a determined little pirouette in the air. He seemed to have a plan. 'At midnight, I want you to come to the gulmohar where we first met. Wear the silver prayer beads for protection. I'll take your leave now. Your mother is approaching.'

The next thing she knew, he'd disappeared.

Chapter 17

The cramping dissipated as soon as Sharmeen put the beads around her neck. She rested in bed reciting the prayers of protection Nani had taught her, wondering what the night held in store for her. When the grandfather clock in the hallway gonged a sombre twelve, she threw back the covers and jumped out, fully dressed, wearing her most comfortable sneakers and two pairs of socks. Nani would have approved. She was a firm believer in double-socked insulation. Many a hero in her stories fought evil sorcerers and rescued princesses only to catch a cold and die in the end. 'All the forces in the world can't combat cold feet and carelessness,' she'd say. Now, going on a perilous trek in the dark to heaven knows where, she figured she'd best follow her grandmother's advice.

She tucked the tassels of the beads under her shirt, and felt shielded by their power. The thought of traversing the darkening corridor was intimidating: in one room lay her father, battling Sargosh, who might get a whiff of her if she lingered too long outside. In the kitchen near the front door was Aziz, a light sleeper who would probably hear her opening the front door.

The only other course available, a significantly more dangerous one, was through her room's window. The banyan was a ghastly but fairly uncomplicated descent. Sharmeen considered her options. The gnarled tips of the branches looked like wooden fingers with sharp nails beckoning her to certain doom. But the weight of the beads around her neck reassured her. She muttered a prayer and slowly opened the window so that it swung inward. She was face-to-face with the banyan.

Dismissing nervous thoughts from her mind, Sharmeen eased herself on the outer ledge, her legs dangling outside. It wasn't a long way down. She reached for the branches. Grabbing hold of the nearest one, she jumped and hung precariously in the air, watching the branch droop with her weight. Terrified that it would snap, she swung herself so that her foot caught in a nook. Mustering strength she didn't know she possessed, she walked her hands along the branch until she was able to grab the trunk. There she clung like a koala bear, willing herself to keep moving, and, as is the case with most leaps of faith, she continued to find firm footholds as she inched down, deep into the recesses of the bearded tree. She reached the branch on which she had seen the woman and sat down on it, using her legs to inch lower. Occasionally she slipped and scraped her elbow or her face against the wizened bark. But the ground approached and she jumped off, tumbling on the ground and scraping her palms and knees.

Bruised, out of breath, but triumphant, she ran towards the gulmohar that seemed like a gentle fairy next to the lurking beast of the banyan. The full moon was partially hidden by grey, luminescent clouds so that the light wasn't clear. But for Sharmeen, the worst was over.

She whispered Jugnu's name and looked around for a firefly, but found none. A rustle in the bushes behind the tree alerted her to his presence. She turned around to see the regal approach of a magnificent peacock, its feathers glistening in the moonlight and its tail spread out in a brilliant display of colour. Small scales like gold coins were huddled together at the base and fanned out into arches of shimmering sapphire. Each feather seemed to display what looked like a little eye, haughtily looking down upon her. The arrogant hook of its nose sliced the night and on its head rested a stately white diamond.

'What a magnificent costume, Jugnu!' exclaimed Sharmeen, clapping her hands together in delight.

The peacock accepted her praise with stoic indifference, but did a little dance, fanning its feathers in the night. And then it let out a hoarse, strangulated cry that made Sharmeen jump.

'Are you okay?' she asked, alarmed.

'Terribly embarrassing,' said Jugnu on behalf of the peacock, folding his feathers. 'A peacock is lovely as you say, but its honking startles even me. The myth goes that the first peacock wailed and lamented because he looked down at his feet and thought that the rest of him was just as offensive. In any case, I sincerely apologize. Note to self: Dance without sound.'

Sharmeen looked down to see the bird's sharp, knobbed talons.

'How come you're a peacock today, Jugnu? It hardly makes you less noticeable.'

'Let's walk, shall we? Why am I a peacock—well, we are going to see the Morpir whose eyes are as blue as my plumage. A tribute, you might say.' Sharmeen fell into step beside Jugnu, whose head jerked forward with every step he took, resembling a serpent striking into the dark—beautiful and evil all at once. And yet she found it much nicer to walk next to a peacock than a dung beetle or a gecko.

It was not an agile creature. It looked fierce, but was encumbered by the weight of its beautiful feathers, trailing behind it like an embroidered train. Even now Jugnu was walking gingerly, trying not to keel over on his own weight. They reached the front gate and Sharmeen allowed him to saunter outside first. She closed it behind her with a loud clang and winced, afraid that even the slightest sound would alert Aziz, or her mother, or the woman. Or Sargosh.

The thought of Sargosh spooked her and she hurried next to Jugnu, who walked down a narrow sidewalk next to the main road. Not a single creature or person was in sight. Only the phosphorescent yellow of the street lamp lent a comforting series of halos to light their path. It had been a long time since Sharmeen had left the house for a purpose other than school. Her mother had stopped socializing after her father's accident, choosing instead to lock herself in the house. In that moment, Sharmeen realized that there were different types of possession. Sometimes, you didn't even need a Jinn to trap you in your body; all you needed were your own fears and superstitions to hedge you in, keep you from the world.

Take Nani, for instance. Wonderful Nani with her fantastic stories and her will of steel, who despite her strength, never left the house. She was obsessed with omens and signs of doom and was trapped in the anticipation of evil. Amir had once commented on Nani's inability to leave the house. 'Some people make their own prisons, Sharmeen,' he had said when she'd asked him why Nani never visited them. 'Nani's very happy in the one she's constructed for herself.' Her poor father, he was imprisoned too, but without his consent.

'Jugnu, is Abba in a lot of pain?'

'I don't think he's in physical pain, little one. But the way a Qarin works is insidious. He keeps your father alive through the terror of his worst nightmares. The nightmares create fear that gets the blood pumping, which Sargosh sniffs and lives off. He frightens him only enough to drain him.'

'So Abba is not in pain. He's just frightened and tired.'

'Indeed.'

'Which is sort of like pain, isn't it?'

'Yes.'

Sharmeen remembered the way she had felt when she saw the woman on the banyan. She didn't want to think about her father feeling like that for such a long time. And yet, how strong he must be, how much of a fighter that he was continuing to survive.

'Jugnu, have you ever wondered why Sargosh does what he does? I mean, he could have moved somewhere else once Aabid decided to build our house. He didn't have to trap the Janeeree, he didn't have to do this to my father...I don't see the sense in so much revenge.'

'The mischief-maker has no motive other than to torment: that is the way of Satan. Sargosh loves suffering, he feeds on it. He has received nourishment from the Rejected One the way a baby bird receives food from its mother. He cannot survive without it. He doesn't need a purpose. That's the thing about evil: it is usually senseless.'

'You know, Jugnu, I used to think that Aziz was evil, but...I don't think he is.'

'Why is that?'

'Because the day I saw the woman, he was so kind, so understanding. I think he's suffering too.'

Jugnu paused to give Sharmeen a searching look, as if he were peering into her memories.

'I think, Sharmeen, that one should not be so quick to label a person as good or bad. As I've told you before, the best of people have a little evil inside them, the most evil have a little bit of good. The wisdom lies in seeing a *whole* person, not just a part of them.'

Sharmeen remembered her grandmother, so fierce and callous towards Aziz, but so loving and protective towards her. And Aziz, always interfering, yet still kind. And the Janeeree, who destroyed a man's life but also her own self to save another. It didn't make any sense, but perhaps it wasn't supposed to. Perhaps that was the strength of a spirit, be it human or Jinn: the ability to change and choose for the best, even when the choice went against nature and expectation.

'I have come to a conclusion about Aziz,' said Jugnu. 'He has been a mystery to me from the beginning. I can't hear him and now I know why.'

Sharmeen looked at him expectantly but realized he wasn't planning to finish the thought.

They had reached a dead end, blunting out to the edge of a tall white wall painted with lewd images and graffiti: a man and a dog with enlarged testicles, a burqa-clad woman emerging from a puff of smoke.

'Well now,' came Jugnu's deep voice, 'our *walk* is over— which is just as well because this creature is perfect for travel by air.'

Sharmeen felt tendrils of nervousness creep over the back of her neck, but she waited patiently and after a few minutes saw a giant falcon fly towards her, majestically silhouetted against the white cloud. It landed on the ground and focused its sharp, intelligent, hook-nosed gaze at her. Its eyes were pools of liquid gold, and a black wedge spread over its head and on its cheeks. The crowned peacock seemed downright frivolous to this magnificent warrior bird with feathers speckled in brown and black.

'Hello again!' Sharmeen said, smiling. 'I think I like you best as a falcon. I think you have the spirit of a falcon.'

Jugnu spread his wings and executed a smart bow. 'Thank you. I think so myself. Now, are you in the mood for a ride?'

She looked at the bird in front of her. Though majestic, it would be crushed under her weight. So no, she wasn't in the mood.

'Have some faith, will you? I'm going to do something that may alarm you, but Jinn do it all the time. Did you hear about the schoolmaster whose services some Jinn wished to employ?'

Sharmeen shook her head. She blinked, and it seemed to her that the size of the falcon had increased marginally post-blink.

'Well,' continued Jugnu as he increased in dimensions. 'There was a schoolmaster who taught geography at a local village near Haripur. Now, a family of Jinn lived on top of the school building and the parents accosted him, asking him to teach their young as well. The schoolmaster was used to unexpected creatures and strange requests. He allowed them to attend classes on the condition that the Jinn take the shape of human children and behave normally.'

Sharmeen crossed her arms patiently, noticing that in the course of the story so far, the falcon had increased to twice its size.

'The Jinn agreed and their children became pupils. But inevitably, one got bored and decided to play a prank on a little girl and showed her his "trick", growing his hand to the size of a football as she watched in dismay.'

By this point, Jugnu's falcon had quadrupled in size, so that it was almost the size of a baby donkey.

'As you might imagine, the schoolmaster was quite upset and decided to expel his recalcitrant pupil.'

Sharmeen laughed and noticed that the falcon had stopped growing. 'What did the Jinn parents do?'

'Oh, they were reasonable and agreed to take their son out of class. He took his revenge by peeing on the heads of the rest of his classmates who played outside during recess. And they would have been angrier if they'd found out that Jinn-pee on the head would make them go bald before they hit their twenties.'

'Jugnu, were *you* the student?'

'What do you think?' asked Jugnu, his amber eyes glowering at her.

'I think you were.'

'Well, I'm flattered that you think I'm such a rebel. Now, if you don't mind, hop on, so we can go meet Morpir.'

Sharmeen approached the falcon, using conversation to distract her from the tendrils of dread uncurling in her stomach. 'So this is what Jinn can also do? Change size?'

'Indeed. Though I can't grow much bigger than this— but the Ifrits! Oh they can grow to the size of mountains!'

'What are Ifrits?' asked Sharmeen as she circled the falcon, trying to determine a foothold.

'Thoroughly unpleasant individuals. Spoil sports, really. They're bullies who, when they don't get their way, sulk in graveyards and ruins for centuries. And they take their anger out on men who stumble upon these godforsaken areas. But they're very strong and useful: King Suleiman built his famed mines with an army of them. They'd been chained by God to do His bidding. They have this weakness: it's easy to snare them through magic because they are often quite stupid. You hear of Jinn being trapped in lamps—well, only one was, and he happened to be an Ifrit caught in the wrong place at the wrong time. And speaking of wrong places, you can't put your heel there! You'll fall off. And kill me in the process.'

Sharmeen was clambering on Jugnu's back, but finding it awkward. It was like going on piggy-back against a prickly hair-shirt.

'Sharmeen, you're throttling me.'

'Well you should have thought of that before you changed into a falcon, Jugnu. Can't you become a unicorn or a flying cushion or something that's more comfortable to sit on?'

'You humans are never satisfied,' said Jugnu, hopping about, dislodging Sharmeen so she fell on the ground. 'And clumsy at that. Now, see this place, right here?' He spread his wings to expose a concave juncture just where his wings began. 'You put your feet here and dig in. And hold on to my feathers. And don't sit up, lie down. That's how you ride a falcon.'

'It's not like they teach this stuff at school,' said Sharmeen, brushing the dust off her bum. She grabbed a fistful of feathers, ignoring Jugnu's grunt, and straddled his back.

'Well they should; it's more interesting than all the useless things you have to learn by heart. Lean against me. Don't sit up!'

And she obeyed, instantly feeling a lot more settled. She rested her head against the back of his neck, inhaling the scent of wood and old leaves.

Jugnu spread his wings and flapped vigorously. One hop, two and off he went. Sharmeen leaned closer, squeezing her eyes shut, alarmed that her body was in danger of slipping downwards as he climbed the sky. She dug her knees firmly in his side and managed to hold on. The wind and mist blurred her vision, but she didn't want to rub her eyes. She didn't think Jugnu would let her fall, but he'd made it clear that the hanging on was her responsibility.

Many storybooks contain reports of how fabulous it is to fly on a magical being, but as Sharmeen found out, it is a deeply uncomfortable process. Her neck hurt, as did her knees and when she did manage to open her eyes, all she saw was darkness. Moreover, the proper hairstyle during an uncovered flight is a bun or a tight pony tail. Sharmeen's untied locks pricked her eyes and tickled her nostrils, which she couldn't do much about because she was too busy holding on for dear life.

Jugnu was silent during their flight, but he flew fast and strong. After what seemed like an eternity, he began to circle the sky, losing altitude with each arc. Upon landing, Sharmeen clambered off, fending off dizziness and nausea, scooping her hair back with one hand and scratching her nose furiously with the other.

'Gather yourself now. I want you to be quiet. We are close.'

Sharmeen was about to ask him where Morpir was, but found herself distracted by the desolation of the landscape. She was on top of a hill that overlooked a small basin, surrounded on all sides by other rocky cliffs. Other than the whistling of the wind, there wasn't any noise. In the centre of the hollow was a huge willow tree—incongruous and unexpected. Jugnu began to descend as Sharmeen followed, getting more nervous by the minute. She wanted to ask him what Morpir was like but had a feeling that words would disrupt the solemnity of the scene.

The willow stood tall, proud and dark, its branches dangling low, the tips almost touching the ground. And as they rounded the edge of the basin, Sharmeen saw him. Morpir: the son of the Janeeree and the hapless Samarkand who had sacrificed his life for him. He sat cross-legged, his white robe luminescent against the dark tree; glowing like a full moon in a black sky. Even sitting down, it was easy to see he was uncommonly tall. His hands rested on his knees—green veins prominent against alabaster skin. His hair, also white, fell in silky strands, ending just above his waist.

Awestruck, Sharmeen waited for Morpir to acknowledge her presence, but he seemed to be in a trance. Suddenly, his eyes opened, blue as the deepest ocean and the darkest sapphire. His liquid gaze held her in an embrace that took as much as it gave. She instinctively knew he understood her situation, that he would help, and the fear that had intertwined its insidious fingers around her person was loosening its hold. She felt free.

Unexpectedly, the gaze transported her into Morpir's past—just as she had been taken into Aabid's. In the span of a few moments, she saw the journey that he had made to become who he was.

She saw a small albino wandering naked in a forest, his blue eyes squinting at the distress of the merciless sun. She saw him scooped up by Kali Daarhi—practitioner of black magic—and carried into a small cottage. She heard cries of distress and the sound of vicious beating, she saw bloodied canes and whips and the red-hot anger of a cruel master who tied a small child with heavy chains, unwilling to let it go, using its blood and tears to concoct the most terrible of potions.

She saw a shivering teenager, a bald runaway high on heroin, his white lashes stark against scarlet cheeks. He skulked in the shadow of a saint's shrine, huddled with other wretched souls, stooping to the ground, injecting himself with golden liquid to forget.

She saw an orange-robed beggar carry the unconscious boy to his hut. She saw him crush red ants in a bowl and rub them on Morpir's eyes. She heard the boy howl and squirm on the ground, covered in his own faeces. She saw him wake up, his eyes blue as the ocean meeting the sky and look, as if for the first time, at the world he was born to be privy to.

She saw him gaze through bloodshot eyes at the home of the earliest Jinn. She knew he gazed at the emerald peaks of Qaf—now aware that they were his destiny. She saw him being led to a small gutter by the beggar and pushed inside, thrown headlong into the tunnel burrowing down into the jewelled cities of Shadkuman: provinces of pleasure and delight that no drug-induced haze could replicate.

Sharmeen saw an older man crawling through the dark

tunnel, his limbs trembling in the hail and storm that he endured for years on end, past the ice and snow. When he could no longer support his weight, he dragged himself by the elbows, collapsing only when he emerged after ten years in a meadow so pristine and sunlight so bright that it shone like silver on his pale skin.

And then he saw the Sultan of the Jinn—a gigantic spirit with a fierce and beautiful bird, the last Phoenix, perched on his shoulder. Sharmeen saw the young Morpir reach out, asking for salvation. Trembling and doubling over, he was flung onto the ground again and again till she heard his bones crack. She felt the pain of Morpir's purification—the opening of his chest and the bleeding of his heart; the transference of fire and his transformation into an Amluq.

And finally, she saw Morpir as he was now, not old, not young, traversing the world; his eyes sometimes blue, sometimes glowing like the embers of a dying fire—corrupted by humans and purified by Jinn.

These eyes now turned to gaze at Jugnu who had flown in behind Sharmeen, a peacock once more. Morpir smiled and bowed his head in graceful acknowledgement. 'It is unfortunate that I am not associated with a less inconvenient creature, my old friend,' he said, his voice deep with restrained laughter. 'And though it is hard for you to sustain your current form, I thank you for the trouble of assuming it.'

Jugnu did not reply, but merely bowed his head.

'And this is Sharmeen. Descendent of Aabid,' said Morpir, looking at her.

Sharmeen nodded. 'Yes, I am.'

She paused, not knowing what to say next. The polite thing to do would have been to thank Morpir for the sacrifice his mother had made for her ancestor, but somehow, it didn't seem appropriate.

Morpir smiled in a way that made Sharmeen suspect that he had heard her thoughts.

'Your grandmother was a great woman, a friend of the Jinn and wise in the mysteries of the world.'

'Nani used to tell me stories about you. I...just want to say that I'm very glad to meet you. Jugnu said that you could help us and now I have a feeling that he's right.'

'Ah, so you're a wise girl, not taking the words of a Jinn at face value. They're clever tricksters, did you know?'

'Jugnu is my friend.'

Morpir smiled and beckoned her close, indicating that she should sit beside him, under the willow. As she complied, he said, 'That is true. He is a good friend to all who have the fortune of earning his loyalty.'

Morpir turned his deep gaze on her. His eyes skimmed the silver prayer beads around her neck. 'It has been some time since I saw this gift to the Watchers of your family. I'm glad it has been protected. Tell me, do you feel safe with it?'

Sharmeen nodded. 'How come these beads are so powerful?'

'Each time my grandmother threaded a bead on this string, she prayed that her son would be protected from the calamities of the world, knowing full well that he would abandon her one day. My father gifted it to my mother in her time of need, despite her abuse and torment of him—so she could defend me. They are the product of love and inspire it, guarding all who wear them.'

'My father loves us,' whispered Sharmeen and Morpir understood.

'Yes, and that is why he holds on. Remember: true love is like the purest of flames of smokeless fire. It can never be extinguished. It is born out of a great strength: a willingness to fight, to battle and to suffer. That is why you will see that the greatest of lovers seem fierce and rough—they have little softness—for love is something that only the soul of a warrior possesses.'

'Like your mother. She—she sacrificed herself for us.'

Morpir seemed to start, as if he had not expected such a candid answer. 'An old soul. You have the wisdom of your ancestors.'

He got up and walked a few paces and then looked back at Sharmeen. 'Yes, like my mother, who had to have the same sinister mettle to fight the evil of Sargosh. Without it, she would have been vanquished much faster than she was.'

Looking at his bowed head, Sharmeen felt guilty. 'I'm sorry I brought her up, I shouldn't have.'

'No. It is good that her sacrifice is with you—which you will pass on to your children and children's children, so that she continues to live in your words. She will not live if Sargosh wins. And for Sargosh to lose, your father must die. For Aziz to win, again, your father must die. Is that not the way of it?'

'I cannot read Aziz's thoughts, Wise One,' interjected Jugnu, 'because Sargosh whispers to him constantly and Aziz listens.'

'Yes,' said Morpir, 'for only one Jinn can occupy the mind of a man. It was Sargosh's whisperings that brought murder upon the land. But Sargosh is weak because the father fights him—as does Aziz, who is sometimes free of him and sometimes not. Her father cannot survive. His body is too frail even if his soul is not.'

'Morpir,' Sharmeen interrupted, 'What do you mean that Aziz is not completely free of Sargosh?'

'In his moments of weakness—full of hate and despair— Aziz is an easy target for a Qarin, especially one as enervated as Sargosh. It is easy to whisper to a person already trapped in longing, sadness and hatred.'

'It seems, sometimes, that my mother is also possessed,' Sharmeen confessed.

'She is not possessed by Sargosh, no. What weakens her is despair, which is a more dangerous foe, taking root slowly until it blooms: full and devastating, strangling the heart. Your mother is not as strong as you or your grandmother. Aziz's presence weakens her; we learn to stand on our own when there is no one to lean on. For her, despair is the demon within. And for us, Sargosh is the demon without.'

'But how do we save my father, Morpir? Jugnu says that you will know a way. Tell me that there's a way!' Sharmeen implored, grabbing his robe with both her fists, her eyes tearing up.

Morpir gently placed his hands on hers and calmed her. 'Yes, there is, but it will require great courage from you.'

'I swear I won't be afraid.'

'Ah, but you will face fear, and you will learn to conquer it. I am not a seer; I cannot guarantee that your father will come out alive. You are also not safe, because once Sargosh leaves your father, your body will be the first that he will be drawn to. Do you understand all this?'

Sharmeen nodded.

'That any attempt to exorcise Sargosh will place you in danger.'

'But then how do I protect myself?'

'With this,' said Morpir, reaching into his robes, to take out a hand made of iron, its five fingers pointed in the air—thin as a blade and just as sharp. She heard a hiss from Jugnu.

'I apologize, my friend, for the lack of warning. I forget how painful iron can be for you.'

'There is no offense taken,' said Jugnu, this time from a greater distance.

Morpir looked at Sharmeen. 'This is the hand of truth, valour and righteousness. It has been made from the legendary sword of Azoth, forged by an ancient alchemist, fashioned from mercury and meteorite iron. It can slice through any substance—even the smokeless fire of Jinn. When this blade slices through Jinn, they are wounded. It can hurt, but not kill them. You must defend yourself with it.'

But Jugnu's voice cut in abruptly. 'Do you know what you ask of her?'

The clapping of thunder punctuated Jugnu's protests and Sharmeen shivered, a feeling of dread overtaking her.

'Sargosh is weak and this girl is a young woman who has withstood more than any child her age can. She is a warrior, though she has not discovered it yet.'

'She is still young!' protested Jugnu.

'And she must have your strength when she fights the battle that is written in her palms. Do not let your protection weaken her.'

Their interchange left Sharmeen dizzy with fear. She looked at her hands, the deep lines that formed a half moon in the centre of her palm. 'Morpir, tell me what is going to happen.'

His face softened and he led her to a mound under the open sky where dark clouds had begun to gather.

'Tomorrow night, I will come to your house. It is imperative that you be the only person in the room apart from me. Sargosh will be made to leave your father's body.'

Sharmeen shivered. 'You'll perform an exorcism?'

'Yes, and while Sargosh is busy with you, Jugnu will try to release your father from the dark prison in which Sargosh has him cornered and entrapped. Whether your father's body will survive, I cannot say. An exorcism is exhausting; it wreaks havoc on a human.'

Sharmeen nodded. 'And then, what about me?'

'Sargosh will have plenty of time to entrap you. You have many fears and nightmares—he will use them to cage you in. I want you to fight as hard as you can with this blade, injure Sargosh so that he is further weakened such that it is easy to extricate him from your body. He will be too weak to fight me, needing easier prey. And he will choose this.' Morpir took out a small vial filled with a deep red liquid. 'It is fresh blood, and Sargosh will come after it: He is a creature of impulse and appetite.'

Sharmeen shivered. 'So I am to be bait?'

'A necessary one. Sargosh will not leave your father's body for any other reason but that he has a more pleasurable host. You are the key.'

Sharmeen nodded and tried to feign a courage that she did not feel. Morpir placed his hand on her head in gentle benefaction, knowing that words could not comfort her.

'Tomorrow at midnight, then, brave warrior of the Watchers. You've had a long journey and have a longer one yet. Sleep will give you strength and these beads will guard you from nightmares. Go.'

Sharmeen turned to find Jugnu, but Morpir smiled. 'I have an easier way to send you back. Courage be with you.'

He closed her eyes and muttered. In an instant, the basin, the willow tree, Jugnu and the night sky faded away. Sharmeen felt a dizziness consume her. The landscape seemed to fly past. Mountains and clouds fell away to reveal a road and a lamp post and then her garden and then her window, and before she knew it, she was in bed, socks and sweaters and all. Overwhelmed, she welcomed the sleep that forced her eyes shut and led her to a dreamless place.

Chapter 18

On the first day of her thirteenth year, Sharmeen was woken up by her mother's hug and a birthday song. She listened irritably, trying not to snap at her earnest parent, who was unaware of Sharmeen's night-journey on the back of a prickly falcon and the exorcism that was to take place in a few hours.

'Why don't you invite your friends home today? I could make some sandwiches. Aziz is baking a lovely velvety chocolate cake for you.'

'I don't want to.'

'It'll cheer you up.'

'I just don't want a party, okay? I'm late for school,' snapped Sharmeen, disappearing into the bathroom to avoid further discussion. Aliya sighed, not saying much when her daughter skipped breakfast. *Thus began her teenage years,* she thought as she watched Sharmeen shrug her boulder of a bag on to her shoulders and stomp off, leaning forward to carry its weight more easily.

***

School was tiresome, especially since it was her birthday and no one knew because she hadn't really told anyone about it. She didn't have any friends to tell anyway so it really shouldn't have mattered. Still, she felt vaguely victimized and neglected. A double period of Math cemented her despair. The recess was spent in the library, again, all alone, watching the ticking of the clock, wishing it would slow down because she wasn't looking forward to what the night held in store for her.

The hot bus-ride home didn't make things better; neither did the cake Aziz had baked for her, nor Aliya's insistence that she should at least *try* to enjoy the day because it was important to celebrate the good times.

Only when darkness descended and everyone retired to their rooms did Sharmeen have time to stop being irritated. Vexation was replaced by deepening dread.

Ten o'clock found her jittery and unable to sit down.

Eleven o'clock saw a deep terror crawl over her like a tenuous vine, blooming into throat-clogging fear at the gong of midnight. It was only then that she realized she'd been gripping Nani's prayer beads so hard that her knuckles had turned white.

Crouching underneath her bed, she called out frantically for Jugnu.

'I'm here,' came the soft reply. 'It is time.'

His voice made her feel better. Less alone. She got up from the floor and took a steadying breath. Turning the door knob, she walked into the dark hallway.

'Don't be afraid,' said Jugnu, appearing as a firefly,

lighting up the way so she could see patterns of leaves and tendrils on the white Persian rug beneath her feet. 'Everyone's fast asleep. You're in the clear.'

Taking one unsteady step at a time, Sharmeen walked towards her father's room. It was a battle of instinct and will—every fibre of her being was pushing her to run away, but she willed her heavy limbs to keep moving forward.

This is for Abba, she told herself.

When she reached Amir's door, the heaviness lifted, and an invisible force began drawing her in. She pulled back, her arms taut, head averted, her body aslant, like a herring caught in a trawl. Her presence had been detected. Her heart started pounding.

'Don't resist,' whispered Jugnu. 'Let it happen.'

The door opened and Sharmeen was sucked in. The window was closed. There was no one else in the room except her dad. Her grandmother's prayers and charms for protection slipped away as she was lured closer to her father's body, like an unwilling child being swept into an adult's perverse embrace. Her head spun. In the silence her words came out loud and abrupt. 'I'm here. Stop!'

A tingle and a prick at the back of the neck alerted her to the presence. She stiffened, and whirled around to see the cloaked woman in the corner, jeering and cackling. But this was no apparition: She was real this time, the height and size of her grandmother. Her gummy smile close to Sharmeen's face, her breath smelling like putrid flesh. Wrinkled nostrils flared as she sniffed her hair.

'What a delicious little duckling has waddled into our lair. And how wonderful it smells. It needs to be eaten!'

Sharmeen stood frozen as the crone did a little hop and dance, reaching out but pulling away just before her gnarled fingers touched her smooth arm. She leaped and leered, her movements wild and hysterical. She jumped up high and her arms caught the fan with incongruous dexterity and she scuttled along the ceiling, hanging just above her prey's head. Suddenly, with a manic shriek, she plunged, gnarled fingers curled like the talons of a crow. Sharmeen was transfixed by the horror of her, unable to move.

And yet, the crone couldn't get anywhere near her. Her nails stopped just a fraction above Sharmeen's head and she let out a guttural cry of despair as she flung herself back to the corner of the room again. Around Sharmeen's neck, the silver beads gleamed in the blue rays of the moon that was beginning to emerge from behind grey clouds.

The shutters of the window flew open and a white dove flapped in, making straight for the woman who seemed to tremble before disappearing. Sharmeen felt a hand on her shoulder and she gasped and turned around, stifling her scream. Morpir had finally arrived.

His blue eyes narrowed as he concentrated on the corner where the creature was.

'So he manifests as an old witch. Appropriate for a Qarin who has lived off the mortification and shame of a thousand women in his day.' His eyes flashed in fury at the memory of his dead mother.

He swivelled abruptly and walked towards Amir, his robe flapping furiously behind him. The vial of blood was placed next to the bed. He opened a book with a gleaming silver cover.

'It is time,' he said. 'Jugnu, you are needed now, my friend.'

A gust of cool wind blew on Sharmeen's face.

Morpir held out his palm to her. After a moment's confusion, she realized what he was asking her to do. She took off her beads and handed them to him. And as she did so, Amir started breathing even more heavily.

'Whatever you see, whatever happens, remember that it is an illusion Sargosh creates to scare you. The only power he has over you is that which you give him.'

Sharmeen nodded and gulped, watching in terror as her father's breathing became more and more laboured. Morpir took her outstretched hand and in it placed the five-fingered iron blade. She clutched it close to her heart, blinking back tears.

He closed his eyes and began to chant ancient prayers of the Amluq that contained the hundred names of God and invocations of His protection. A terrible writhing took over Amir's body: torso twisting, fingers gripping thin air, legs stiffening, back arching so violently that Sharmeen feared he would break his spine.

Morpir took the prayer beads and placed them on Amir's forehead. Her father moaned and Sharmeen's heart broke at how much pain lay in that sound. He turned his head from one side to the other, convulsing. One jerk, two, and the third time he sat up straight, stiff-backed, opening bloodshot eyes that scanned the room but did not see. Sharmeen's heart skipped a beat. This was her father and yet not—it was the monster inside his skin. His head moved in slow jerks and came to rest on her. His smile chilled her to the bone: a slow spreading leer. The tip of a long brown tongue licked the base of his chin.

Morpir continued his prayers—the whites of his eyes rolled back, making it seem like he too had been possessed. His incoherent mutterings formed a monotonous backdrop to the fearful sight of Amir's slow turning head as he stared at Sharmeen, smile contorting into a scowl. His eyes darted suspiciously between Sharmeen and Morpir, torn between the safety of a worn out shell and the dangerous temptation of a newly bled woman. She enticed him like an oasis in the desert.

Sargosh's longing for her grew so potent that Sharmeen was caught in its tide—the stirrings of a warm feeling tickled the base of her stomach. Her limbs gave way to a delicious relaxation. She felt a thousand little butterfly wings fluttering inside, tantalizing her, making her yearn for concrete touch. Images began to swirl in her head, leaving her disoriented, hammering upon her brain: visions of midnight sky and darkening dunes. Her father faded, as did the room, Morpir and all the dangers she felt were imminent, leaving her with a delicious sensation, like a dip in cold water after a long hot day. She wanted to sink deeper and deeper.

And as she sank, Sargosh rose, triumphant out of Amir's wracked body. Her scent was sweet as nectar, as tempting as the blue sky of day to a prisoner who had been trapped too long in the gloom.

'I shall take her, you shall not get her back,' Sargosh

hissed at Morpir as he emerged in a spiral of black cloud that drew inexorably upon the slender, defenseless little girl in the middle of the room. Morpir stopped chanting, his eyes turning red, and an enigmatic smile spread on his face as he watched Sargosh consume his new host.

Chapter 19

She was sinking in quicksand. It muttered and gurgled like an old woman choking on porridge. Sharmeen struggled, trying to yell for help, but no sound came. She tried to wade out but the more she moved, the more she sank into the ground. Soon the muck was just beneath her nostrils. She panicked and flailed her arms in the air, and her wrist came into solid contact with something.

Veined, slender hands, ghostly white, clasped her arms and pulled her out. They belonged to a woman with brilliant blue almond-shaped eyes, her hair thick and long like the leaves of a weeping willow. The Janeeree placed a long, slender finger on her lips. She turned and walked away, indicating with a nod of the head that she should be followed.

But she walked too fast for Sharmeen to keep up. A sudden breeze swept up the leaves around her retreating form and whipped up into a tornado. Sharmeen tried to shout a warning to the Janneree, but her lips seemed to be sealed; she couldn't open them. The tornado snuffed the figure of Janeeree and turned towards her. Strong gusts pushed and pulled at her body, leaving her curled on the ground.

Black clouds were beginning to gather. A terrible clap of thunder, sharp as a whip, made her jump. Again it came and again, chiding her, threatening death by fire. Sharmeen ran to a banyan that had loomed up beside her, sinister and solitary. Its vines moved like snakes to reveal a small opening. Another crack of thunder and the clouds bled, rain slashed against her, each drop like a needle piercing her skin.

There was no option. Sharmeen crawled inside, pulling herself through the narrow opening into the silence within. The vines, slithering like worms, closing off the opening, leaving her trapped inside. She reached out for the solid feel of wood, but it eluded her, her fingers grasping air. Crawling on the ground, she tried to find something that could afford her some solidity in the dark. And yet she touched nothing, just an all-encompassing blackness that yielded only more of itself.

But even the dark has some colour. Images began to stir in flashes that became larger and closer to reveal many scenes.

The fall of a slab of cement.

Nani's crushed skull.

Aziz digging up a grave and cutting a dead child's hair.

Aliya grabbing Aziz in a passionate embrace.

Amir writhing in pain, screaming in agony.

Morpir and Jugnu, circling Sharmeen, tall and menacing.

'Please stop! I can't see this anymore!' she pleaded, trying to close her eyes but they were already shut.

A snickering laugh right behind her was quickly followed by strong fingers clasping her shoulders.

'There, there,' a voice crooned, 'Do not struggle, little one. Take my hand, I'll take you somewhere safe.'

'Take your hands off me!' yelled Sharmeen, jerking herself away and turning around.

'Poor little girl doesn't know friend from foe. She is in danger, though not from me.'

Sharmeen blinked back tears. 'I don't understand.'

Sargosh frowned briefly, and said, 'I have a question for you. Who is the real whisperer of lies?'

Sharmeen's brow furrowed in confusion. Sargosh's voice was changing—it was no longer thick and sweet, but deep and clear.

Sargosh paced before her, shaking his head in disappointment. 'Little woman has no chance against a liar like my old friend. What does he call himself? Jugnu? Filthy little firefly, telling you lies, killing a man and accusing *me* of it, telling you that I am the enemy.'

'You *are* my enemy,' said Sharmeen, 'I saw you possess my father.'

'Tsk tsk, you saw what your "friend" showed you,' came the silky reply. 'It is true that I was inside your father, holding on to his soul that tries to fly away. Here's another question: What happens to a body without a soul? Ah, you understand. Had it not been for me, little girl's father would have died a long time ago.'

Sharmeen shook her head, unable to think straight.

Still Sargosh whispered, 'Ask yourself who kept your father alive, when everyone else wanted to kill him. Whose story do you believe? A shape-changer who hides in small animals, a glow-worm who got to the little girl while Sargosh was too busy trying to keep her father alive? Does not the girl see how he strikes a deal with the blue-eyed devil to trap me inside her, to imprison me with your body? They have filled the girl's head with lies.'

'J-Jugnu is my friend,' said Sharmeen, her voice hesitant.

'So he must appear to be, to earn your trust. Tell me, how do you know his visions are true? He shows you pretty mirages. I am his enemy, this was my land. The Janeeree, evil, despicable Spider-Fangs, *she* took *my* land. I grappled with her, trapped her here so she could no longer kill innocent men that wandered into her lair. Has little one thought about her blue-eyed friend, who consorts with creatures of the night and mourns a mother who has inhaled the souls of a thousand travellers?'

A slow dread crept upon Sharmeen. What he said made sense—he could just as well be telling the truth.

'Poor little girl has been tricked. Take my hand and I will show you what *really* happened: how Jugnu and Morpir contrive to trap my powers for their use—how they use pretty sweet little girls and make them their pets. That's right, take it: I shall make everything alright.'

Sharmeen looked at his hand—pointed and blue as the dying flames of candle light. She didn't know whom to trust. Morpir, the son of an evil she-demon? Jugnu—who came from god-knows-where and who may just have befriended her in the loneliest of times to manipulate her? Or this despicable creature, who might be caught in a web of lies, or the weaver of the web itself? She just didn't know.

Sargosh was getting impatient. 'Come, there is not enough time. Let me show you the truth.'

Uncertain and scared, she didn't resist when Sargosh slid his hand onto her palm. She just wanted to get out of this place. He grasped her hand and smiled. Bending down, he whispered in her ear, just as his other arm curled around her shoulders. 'Delicious little ducky, don't be afraid. We will take care of her.' He brought his face closer to hers, his lips just above her mouth, his breath smelling like the gutter. 'Let me in, little ducky. I will let no one hurt you.'

It was his leer that made her resist. The yellow teeth and brown tongue that licked them reminded her of the witch who had tried to attack her. Sharmeen pulled away and Sargosh laughed, curling his palm around her shoulder. 'Ducky wants to run. There is nowhere to go. I've got hold of you now.'

She jerked away and bit his hand, pushing past him to run deeper into the darkness. Sargosh laughed and chased after her. His hoarse guttural voice was close behind her. 'She gives us chase! How exciting! Does silly little ducky not know she can't escape?'

Something caught her foot and she collapsed on the ground. A sharp object pierced her skin just below her chest. She hissed in pain. Underneath her clothes, she felt the iron hand safely tucked under her belt. Sargosh loomed over her, grabbing her left arm and pulling her up, roughly. In the blink of an eye, she took out the blade of Azoth and slashed his face. A nasty gash slanted from his forehead to his upper lip. He howled and let her go, burying his face in his palms. Black smoke rose from his wound. Sharmeen stared as he turned to face her once more and hissed at her. Pouncing on her, he clamped her hands on the ground. The blade disappeared.

'You cannot hurt me,' she said, 'you are in my mind. I will not let you hurt me.'

Sargosh snickered and brought his face close to hers. 'If we are in your mind...*where did the hand come from? How did you injure me?*'

He stuck out a long toad-like tongue and licked her cheek. Sharmeen screamed.

'I can do whatever I like,' he said menacingly, 'Because I have finally got hold of you.'

Sharmeen squirmed and struggled, panic rising like bile in her throat. She bucked but could not throw Sargosh off. His clammy hands descended upon her and she knew at this moment that she was lost, pinned down and helpless. A terrible sense of hopelessness flooded her. There was to be no salvation this time, no twist in the tale. Her time was over, as her grandmother's had been and her father's before her. She saw her future: dank and endless pathways of scum and filth stretching out like destiny. Lying on the ground, Sharmeen now understood what it was to just let go of everything, to surrender to wretchedness and misery. How easy the journey became when one reached the end of the road.

She saw Sargosh lean on top of her and inhale and she felt herself beginning to fade.

So this was what it was like to die. A lethargy creeping beneath the thighs, permeating the legs until numbness prevails, the soul threatening to slip out. Listlessness travelling down the calf and to the toes. The hammer-beat of the heart, like a dying motor, pounding at the rib cage. Death does not come as an ending, but as forgetfulness. All was still. She was free to go.

Just then the manacles on her hands loosened and the darkness before her eyes gave way to the fiery light in the distance that grew larger and larger until she realized it was Jugnu, in the shape of a fiery warrior whose skin glowed bright. Sargosh, who had seemed so strong and potent before, looked like a starved beggar in front of him. Sharmeen lay quietly as Sargosh scampered away into the darkness and she felt Jugnu lift her up.

'You've endured this nightmare long enough, little one. Let's get you out.'

Sharmeen was blinded by bright light that stabbed her eyes. Numbness gave way to agony, which felt far more real and immediate than the lethargy she was succumbing to. She embraced the pain, even though it blurred her vision and made her dizzy. The darkness gave way to a vortex of colour, sound and movement that sucked her in, away from where half-formed trees drowned in lakes of quicksand.

What followed was a gentle darkness, not the inky black of despair but the shadows of slumber. She opened her eyes, waking up.

And blinked.

She was back in her father's room. It was not on the floor she lay, but in her mother's arms.

Was this another illusion? No, her mother's arms were real, as were her tears and her terror.

'Amma?' she whispered, reaching up to Aliya's face. But Aliya didn't look at her—no, her attention was diverted to something else. Sharmeen looked to her side and saw Aziz writhing on the floor in the corner of the room. Sharmeen sat up to find Morpir chanting and holding her father's hands.

Her heart skipped a beat when she saw her father open his eyes with a searching look.

He was awake. Amir was back.

Chapter 20

12:30 a.m.

Aliya awoke with a jolt, registering the quiet night and thick darkness. She'd had the nightmare again, but this time it was her daughter and not Amir who screamed in agony, subsumed by the dark fall into the abyss.

She rubbed her throbbing temples, tried to lie back down, but sleep eluded her. A nagging suspicion that something was deeply wrong made her toss and turn, until she decided the only way to silence the voice in her head was to get up and make sure everything was alright. Throwing off the covers, she walked to Sharmeen's room and opened the door, only to find the bed empty. Panic began to set in. Where could she be at this time of the night?

A scream broke the silence. Aliya froze. For one sickening moment, nightmare and reality began to seem as one.

Another scream, from her husband's room.

Choking back a sob, she ran across the corridor calling for Aziz as she went. The light from the kitchen came on. Aziz hobbled out, slightly groggy, putting on his kameez. 'What's wrong?'

Sharmeen screamed again. Aliya struggled with the doorknob. 'It's locked! My baby's inside, Aziz—the door is locked. Open it! Do something!'

Aziz was instantly alert. He ran to get a crowbar as she shoved herself against the door, hoping it would give. 'Sharmeen! Open the door, baby. Let me in!' She hurled herself against the obstinate barrier, desperation giving her renewed strength. Again and again she slammed against it with a will power she didn't know she possessed. After the thirteenth time, the hinges gave way and she stumbled inside. Her gaze flew to the bed and its patient.

No. It couldn't be.

She saw her husband blinking at the ceiling. He was awake. A voice was chanting a prayer, but she could not see where it was coming from. Blood drained from her face as she saw Sharmeen writhing on the floor, frothing at the mouth, the whites of her eyes showing.

Aliya ran to her and drew her convulsing body into a tight hug. She glanced at Amir once again, thinking maybe she'd been mistaken: but no, he was conscious and blinking furiously. She wanted to reach for him, but her daughter's shuddering frame needed immediate attention. 'Aziz! Where are you? Call the doctor! She's having a seizure!'

Sharmeen stopped trembling and fell into a dead faint—only her breathing was an indication that she was not yet dead. A faint whisper reached Aliya's ears. She looked up to see Amir looking at them.

She lay Sharmeen carefully on the carpet and went to her husband. 'Amir? Can you hear me?'

He whispered something—the effort taking all his strength. Aliya bent down and put her ear close to his mouth. 'Leave,' he said. 'Danger.'

Aliya looked at him in consternation. Amir's eyes pleaded with her, he was too weak to say anymore. He looked over her shoulder and she turned around, stifling a scream as she saw a man in a white robe with startlingly blue eyes appear out of nowhere.

'Take these beads. Put them around your neck,' the stranger said.

'Wh-who are you?'

'Now is not the time for questions. Do as I say.'

Aliya stood dumbly, as Morpir placed the beads in her hands and a dark cloak of oily liquid left Sharmeen's nostrils, in search of another host. Sargosh had been vanquished and he searched for a new body once again.

Aliya watched all this in horror. Morpir's iron-grasp prevented her from rushing to her daughter's rescue. A moment later, she was grateful for his support when a wave of dizziness consumed her and she stooped, knees buckling, trying to resist the tickle up the pit of her stomach, like the stroking of a feather inside. Something potent tugged at her, she wanted so badly to succumb to the ecstasy the faint sensation promised.

But the hands that held her up now hurled her violently

on to the ground. She shook her head and looked up to see the white-robed stranger shielding her with his body.

Morpir held up the vial of blood and offered it to the black goop.

'Enter here, Sargosh,' he said.

'I will not!' a hoarse voice hissed.

'You have no choice,' asserted Morpir, grimly.

Just then, Aziz ran inside the room, and a laugh echoed around as the cloud of black enveloped this unexpected host. Aziz doubled over and collapsed on the ground, writhing and smashing his head against the floor so desperately, Aliya feared he would bash his skull. Feeling stronger, she crawled towards Sharmeen and drew her close, cupping the back of her head. Her face was pale and her lips were blue. But it was her hair that startled Aliya: a streak of white ran down it like a bolt of lightning.

Her daughter opened her eyes and looked around.

'What is happening?' she asked Aliya, who responded only by clutching her hard and rocking back and forth. 'Amma, why are you here? You're not supposed to be. What's happening to Aziz?'

Aliya looked down at her daughter. 'I...I heard noises and I came to see and this man...he was praying and you had fainted. There was black, and now, it's in Aziz and I...I must be losing my mind.'

Sharmeen freed herself from her mother's embrace and struggled to rise. Her knees were weak and her head felt heavy, but still, she managed.

The two worlds of fantasy and reality had merged

and she saw them like a revelation: they'd always existed together, intertwining and separating in ways men couldn't yet understand. She hobbled to her father. His eyes recognized his daughter and Sharmeen saw the slight curl of his lips trying a ghost of a smile. She put her hand over his chest and felt a faint, steady heartbeat. Gladness was instantly removed by concern as she looked at Morpir, who solemnly muttered under his breath, his piercing gaze focused on Aziz's trembling form, which was now possessed by Sargosh.

Sharmeen felt her clothes to find the iron hand that had made Sargosh bleed, but it was nowhere to be found. She looked around and found it against Aliya's foot, on the floor. She rushed back to her mother and picked it up.

'Amma,' she said gently, 'Aziz has been possessed by a Jinn. Do you understand what I'm saying?'

Aliya looked blankly at her daughter, her mind too filled with terror to register what she was being told. 'This man here is my friend and he's helped this Jinn leave Abba's body, which is why Abba was unconscious for so long. And now he has entered Aziz. Don't hold these beads, put them around your neck.'

'It is unlikely that Sargosh has the strength to remain in a healthy man's body. Look how they both fight each other even now,' came Jugnu's voice next to her ear, as a firefly wafted in through the window.

Aziz was still trembling, his eyes changing colour with each blink: now red, now yellow, now white. He yelled for help in one moment and hissed at the next—struggling with the creature trying to control him.

'Now is the time to strike,' said Morpir, his voice cold as ice, 'They are both out of control.'

'What do you mean?' Sharmeen asked.

'He cannot influence this body the way he could your father's. Kill Aziz now and you will be rid of Sargosh forever.'

Sharmeen was horrified at the calculating way in which Morpir was circling the man struggling on the floor. His eyes gleamed like a child finally in reach of his plaything. 'My mother's death will be avenged at last.'

Is that why Morpir had agreed to help her? Revenge?

'B-but, that's murder!' she protested. Morpir, however, seemed lost in his own world. 'There has to be another way.'

Morpir glared at her. 'There isn't. Vile monsters like Sargosh do not deserve to live.'

'Who are you to decide?'

Morpir swept down on her. 'I have helped you out of your predicament as promised. Now get out of my way.'

Sharmeen's eyes widened in horror at the crazed, demonic look on Morpir's face as he grabbed her, wrestling the blade of Azoth from her hands. 'Stop it, Morpir! You're better than this! You're hurting me!'

Caught in their struggle, neither noticed Aziz, his eyes now bloodshot, snarl and lunge for Sharmeen. She screamed as he grabbed her braid and yanked her head. Sense seemed to return to Morpir, who lashed out at Aziz and slashed his face with the iron hand. Sobbing, Sharmeen crawled away from both men, hiding behind Aliya who watched with frozen disbelief.

'This close!' hissed Aziz, clutching his face, 'I was this close! And then my enemy stole you away from me.'

He began to crawl towards Sharmeen and Aliya, his tongue licking his lips. He looked at them lasciviously and moved with the slow deliberateness of a komodo dragon.

'Stay away from her!' screamed Aliya, backing away, dragging Sharmeen with her.

Aziz stopped and shook his head and blinked hard. Looking up again, he sat back and reached out, 'Aliya, it's me...help me.'

Aliya moved towards him, but Sharmeen pulled her back. 'No Amma, it's not safe.'

But Aliya lowered her hands. 'Aziz?'

Aziz stood up and walked slowly towards her. 'He's inside me, Aliya!'

'Get him out of you, Aziz,' Sharmeen pleaded, hiding behind her mother. 'You're stronger than him. Jinn can't hold on to grown men for long. Fight him.'

But Aziz had eyes only for Aliya. 'Don't you know me, Aliya Bibi? I'm your Aziz. I've been with you always: I held you when your father and mother died. There is nothing inside, just me. Don't you remember, you asked me to save Sharmeen? Here I am. Let me check if she is okay...'

'No!' screamed Sharmeen, backing away.

Her terror galvanized Aliya, who placed herself between her daughter and Aziz's path. 'That's far enough.'

Her scent galvanized the creature inside. A low menacing growl came from his throat as he cocked his head to look at Aliya. It was the look of a monster, idly assessing this fragile barrier that kept him from his goal. Aliya was terrified, all her mother's warnings and fears had come alive. Sargosh's manic look steeled her resolve. Whatever this thing was, she would not allow it near her daughter. Sharmeen, still traumatized, huddled by the door, hiding. Aliya stepped towards Aziz. 'You will not hurt her,' she said, her voice conveying a steadiness that did not extend itself to her knees.

Aziz snickered and then howled in laughter. 'So you think that you can keep Sargosh—who can whisper into your soul, who can make you do anything he wants—away? Sargosh who has whispered to your servant's body? Sargosh has already tasted your daughter. Now he will taste you too.'

He lunged, his hand grabbing Aliya's face. Sharmeen screamed and saw her mother struggle with him, her body buckling under his super-human strength. He bore down on her and Aliya fell. Morpir charged, stabbing Aziz in the back.

Time stood still. Aziz moaned and fell on his knees. Sharmeen saw the red bleeding away from his eyes. The scowl faded away and black liquid, thick as ink, gushed from his mouth, nose and chest, seeping to the floor in a pool of black, congealed smoke. His body crumpled to the ground. For when smokeless fire mixes with blood, it becomes mortal.

So ended the story of Sargosh.

Aliya sobbed and picked herself up, moving to her old friend, kneeling over him. Aziz looked up at the woman who had once been his friend. The brown of his eyes shone through glimmering tears and greyness spread upon his face. He had returned, only to die. 'I'm sorry, Aziz, I...am so sorry,' she whispered. She held his hands and he clasped her slender fingers.

'Sharmeen?' he whispered hoarsely.

Aliya nodded as Sharmeen clambered towards him. A tear slid from the corner of his eye to his temple.

Aziz looked at the two women whom he had loved so much. He soaked in their two faces and imagined that this was what paradise would have felt like, but as death approached, he knew that heaven was a long way away.

Aliya stroked his check, sobbing silently.

'I'm sorry,' he whispered softly. Aliya shook her head and told him he'd be fine, just as the light left his eyes. Aziz too, was gone.

Chapter 21

Growing up is often tedious—full of slowly passing time and countless moments of nothing. For Sharmeen a few short hours had seemed to shatter life into fragments and she needed to let each dislodged piece find its proper place before things settled down.

The first fragment was laid to rest by Morpir, who carried Aziz to his quarters and laid him down gently on the roped charpoy. Sharmeen had followed, numb, looking at Aziz's lifeless arms dangling beneath Morpir's elbows. A soft spell was muttered and a white hand cast over the bleeding wound to conceal it so that no human eye would ever surmise how he had met his end.

'Tell the world he died in his sleep. Bury him soon,' said Morpir, his blue eyes boring into her soul. Sharmeen nodded, too shocked to realize that Aziz would no longer be around to protect them. She avoided Morpir's gaze— unsure of how to react to him now that his motives no longer seemed as lofty.

Morpir touched her shoulder and said, 'I am proud to help the friends of my mother, and the daughters of the brave woman who had honoured the pact of her ancestors until she was killed for it. You have now been anointed by the Jinn and you shall bear the mark of the Watcher: Soon, your hair will turn completely silver. The veil has lifted from your eyes—it is a gift bestowed upon you from your travails. Let the invisible communicate with you—be unafraid.'

Sharmeen surveyed the silver beads in her hand as if from a distance. After all that had happened, they seemed less magical and more tiresome, much like Morpir himself. She wished he'd go away and leave her in peace. He read her thoughts and smiled enigmatically, 'Peace will come. Eventually.'

And then he faded into the night.

Aziz was buried in the same graveyard as Nani, though a good way off. Sharmeen sprinkled dust on his grave and thought long and hard about him. She remembered Jugnu's words to not judge him—this little boy who sought love and was denied it. If Nani had been kind to him, would he have made the choices that he made? Would Sargosh have taken root in all the emptiness inside him had Nani not created it in the first place? And yet, wasn't her grandmother right to hate him? Hadn't he been the cause of her death? It was dreadfully uncomfortable, this process of sifting through the greys—of not being able to lay the blame unequivocally on one person. Life would be so much more bearable with distinct heroes and villains, but it was not meant to be.

This unpleasant departure from the comfortable cocoon of safety left her feeling older than her years. Her mind was troubled, and the worries of her past seemed frivolous to the troubles in her mind. How silly she had once been, worrying about small things like new schools and awful Math teachers. She almost wished she could go back to that time of naivety.

Her hair was changing colour rapidly, though she didn't pay much notice. She saw and heard much more now. It was as if she'd been sleeping all this time and had only now awakened. The rustles of invisible movement reached her ears, as did the mutterings of Jinn from within the locked store room above her bedroom that was seldom opened. She felt a new life in the trees and grass and the shrubs and the sky—everything was, for her, infused with a new glow. She was responsible for all this, and immensely burdened by it. She hadn't realized just how precious this home was, how full of the mystery that was slowly revealing its secrets to her.

But peace, as Morpir had predicted, did come, slowly. A solidity took root inside her and tightened its clasp, and there mushroomed in her a certainty that no matter what happened, she would survive and endure.

Slowly, she began to find some humour in her new position. The world was crawling with invisible Jinn: some who lived quietly in the trees and others who were fairly eager in making their presence felt. Jinn infants, in particular, had a penchant for riding mice and cockroaches on the ground and pigeons and mynahs in the air, using spiderwebs for hammocks and ceiling fans for swings. They also moved things whenever they felt like it: now opening a door, now rocking her chair, now making sugary water drip from the ceiling on to her head. Sharmeen learned to welcome her new guests, leaving bright trinkets and artificial jewels in nooks and corners, which almost always disappeared the same moment.

As Watcher, she realized that nature was closely aligned with the invisible world, and it was nature she observed early in the morning, just before going to school, making sure that the leaves and flowers were intact. With each passing day, her skills grew—it became easier to decipher the moods of the mynahs that sang in distress if danger was near, or trilled joyously when happy days returned.

The banyan began to die. The gardener didn't know what to make of it. And yet for the seeker of signs as Sharmeen was becoming, it all fit perfectly.

Five men were commissioned to cut it down. It was a rigorous process that took an entire week, but the cause was found soon enough—the roots had rotted and the main trunk had grown hollow. It was carted off in a big truck and the sun shone brightly on the spot, brightening up Sharmeen's room and making the garden seem bigger.

All the while, Sharmeen wondered where Jugnu had disappeared to. Had he abandoned her? She missed him dreadfully. He was the only one she could talk to—the only one who could help her move on—to tell her what was next. If only he'd show up! She watched and waited and listened—but no firefly or gecko or dung beetle surprised her with its deep baritone.

Her parents were also beginning to turn towards life, but they were like children rediscovering their first steps, looking to their daughter for answers. It felt strange to have outgrown her mother and father. Their trust made her feel heavy, even resentful at times. She was too young to take care of them, and yet, that was exactly what she needed to do.

Amir was recovering. He was still terribly weak, but making steady progress, sipping on soups and juices at first, and after a month, managing to sit up for a few minutes. It was hard for Sharmeen to look into his face—still gaunt with sunken eyes, jutting cheekbones and pursed lips. He was too weak to talk and often didn't wish to do so—content to stare at his wife and daughter as if they were a sight he had long given up hope of. And when Sharmeen sat with him, alone in the afternoon, it seemed to her that sometimes he was haunted by the visions that Sargosh had fed him. Sharmeen stayed by him as much as she could. Sometimes he would start awake, gasping for breath and she would rush to his side and whisper, 'It's okay, Abba. You're safe now. He is gone and you are with us.'

When he was strong enough to listen, Sharmeen told him about Aziz and all that had happened since they'd come to this house. It comforted her that he didn't ask any questions or object to an impossible narrative. After all, he had lived for seven months what she had experienced just for a few moments. He needed time, and she was ready to give it to him.

When it came to her mother, Sharmeen felt more

annoyance than patience. Aliya plagued her with questions: how had she found out about the Jinn, why she hadn't told her, why she hadn't warned anyone else? When Sharmeen snapped back, 'Because you were too busy weeping and sleeping, that's why!' Aliya retreated into her shell once again, which angered Sharmeen even more. She was beginning to realize why Nani treated Aliya the way she did: It wasn't a lack of love—no—it was impatience. When one has to be strong on one's own for so long, then another's weakness begins to seem like an irritant, unworthy of attention.

And yet, she had to remind herself of Aliya's bravery during the night of the possession. Sometimes, people surprised you far more than any Jinn ever could.

Time was changing things, but a final piece of the puzzle lay missing for Sharmeen. She called out to Jugnu in her dreams, in her prayers, even through the beads. A month passed, then two, and she began to accept that maybe, like her childhood, he too had disappeared.

One night, when things were especially difficult and memories of Sargosh incredibly potent, she followed in her grandmother's footsteps and stepped out into the garden, no longer bothered by the dark of the night and the flimsy light provided by the flickering lamp post that desperately needed repair. She took off her shoes and stepped on to the lawn, listening to the agitated chirping of the crickets who seemed to be discussing with great excitement some new development in their grassy world.

A wayward breeze caressed her cheek and Sharmeen

turned towards it—it felt like a balm to her agitated mind. She opened her eyes and saw a small firefly suspended in the air, just above her nose, drawing close.

'Where have you been?' she asked with quiet relief. 'I needed you.'

'I know. I came as soon as I recovered,' said Jugnu, perching on her nose. 'Well, little one. I'm proud of you. You did it.'

Sharmeen, who'd been holding her breath, became less pensive. He was here. This was not an illusion. Excitement sprang up inside her as Jugnu hovered close. 'Where on earth were you?'

'I had to fly off for a while, to recuperate. It was a double load operation that night—to possess your father and then you.'

'Yes, I can imagine that must have been exhausting.'

'Oh it was. Though thank heavens both of you smelled quite nice.'

Sharmeen laughed—for the first time after her possession. Joy exploded in her chest. How terribly she'd missed Jugnu! But now he was here and all would be well. There was much to discuss: the new world opening before her, the dying banyan, her role as Watcher. She needed his insights, now more than ever.

Jugnu was also the only one who could tell her about everything that had happened while she had been possessed. She asked him to fill her in on the details.

'The minute Sargosh claimed you, I swooped in to find your father. What a mess had been created in his mind! It took nearly all my strength to navigate his nightmares and search for his real self. And do you know where I found him? In a memory of you stuck in a slide, asking him to pull you out. It was your voice that kept him fighting all this while—he's a brave one. And then when I came out, I was exhausted, but I saw you struggling and I knew I had to help. Sargosh was easy to defeat—his strength had been mostly depleted and he hadn't had enough time to trap you through his illusions. But when I brought you back, I could not stay for long. So I flew to my mountain and bathed in the snow and sunshine and only now have I felt able enough to come back to you.'

'Jugnu, Morpir used me as bait. He wanted revenge. He had *no* compunctions about murdering Aziz.'

'Yes, little one.'

'And you let him.'

'I also knew he would fulfil his promise to you by saving you and your father. But Morpir is an Amluq—he is no saint. He struggles with malice; his battle is a constant one. Yes, he let his viciousness win that night—but it was the same mettle that allowed him to help you in the first place.'

Sharmeen thought about it for a moment. Morpir had come to her aid, but his purposes had also been self-serving. 'I'm so glad you've returned, Jugnu, so that I can discuss these things with you. There's so much I don't get, about Morpir, about myself, about the world.'

Jugnu glowed for a minute. 'I cannot stay.'

'What do you mean?'

'I mean I've come to say goodbye.'

Panic seized Sharmeen, clogging her throat. 'But why can't you stay? If you need to rest, you can rest some more and come back later. I don't mind.'

'I know you don't, but now you have very little need of me. Sargosh is gone and your land is safe. I have atoned for the sins of my youth. My debt to Morpir is repaid. Your parents are back with you. And I see that you now bear the mark.'

Sharmeen stroked her hair self-consciously. 'I suppose so.'

'You fought your battles bravely. You are quite capable of facing anything without my help now.'

'No, I'm not,' interrupted Sharmeen, shaking her head. 'I would never have known about Sargosh or Aziz if it hadn't been for you. I wouldn't have my father back if you had not led me to Morpir. And you were my friend when I most needed one—you helped me so much, Jugnu. I need you. You're my best friend. Don't I mean anything to you? Doesn't our friendship have value enough for you to stay on?'

'Well, this is quite the melodramatic moment! Little one, calm yourself. You are a human and what you have gone through is extraordinary. A journey like the one you've been through could have left any other mortal scarred for life.'

'Well, I am scarred.' Sharmeen held up her braid for closer inspection. 'Jugnu, I am so alone. I can't talk to anyone about what I'm feeling and hearing. Abba just lies there—and I understand why; Amma is better, but neither of them are strong enough for me. I need someone like Nani, or you. It's just too much.'

'I understand. You've had a lot thrust upon you in too short a time. But a new world is awakening around you, is it not?'

'You mean the Jinn? Yes. By the way, some little Jinn stole my Math workbook and then returned it with all the equations neatly worked out. I'm trying to figure out how to get them to do it again. You can help me communicate with them! We can all be one huge family.'

'What will the world think if it finds out that you have not humans, but Jinn for your family?'

'The world doesn't have to know. I don't need it.'

Jugnu glowed for a while, watching her struggle with her emotions. 'But I want you to need the world. It is where you belong. Already, your lot is not easy. Your attention will be drawn to omens and whisperings and premonitions—this is your duty as a Watcher. But you cannot live with my company alone. You need people, ordinary ones. You need to think about everyday humdrum things, like homework and birthday parties and gossip. My presence will take you away from the world of mundane pleasures.'

'I don't care about the world of mundane pleasures,' said Sharmeen obstinately.

'Then why would you ever be moved enough to defend it?'

Sharmeen opened her mouth to argue, but no response came.

'Our world is too tempting for humans, little one. It is

easy to lose yourself in it. But you are needed in this life. Our worlds are apart—mine invisible and remote, yours here and now. It is not natural for us to be together all the time. I will end up frustrated and you, my presence will make you hard.'

'Hard, Jugnu?'

'Yes, hard. In the sense that you will never need anything more to satisfy you. People who court the company of Jinn, who live in our world all the time, they gain too much. We become addictive, drawing humans away from the vulnerabilities of flesh and blood. You will become too complete—not needing to reach out to humans, to understand or help them.'

Sharmeen thought of Nani, dismissed as crazy by the world, rejected by her own daughter, because she had no sympathy for the lives and fears of ordinary folk. Her wisdom made her powerful, but also ruthless.

'I see my words spark an understanding inside that stubborn, intelligent head of yours. Only when the need arises will they intersect and at that time, your gift will guide you. Until then, you must be on your own, and to my world must I retire.'

Sharmeen listened to all this in tears, shaking her head, not wanting to admit the truth of his words. 'It's awful of you to leave just after I've found you. What will I do without you?'

'There are some children who weep just like this when they are very young, when they see and know us. Most grow out of it; until one day, they forget that there was ever a world where they saw the Jinn ride on comets or hover over their cribs at night, trying to make them laugh with their tricks. But some continue to hold on to us and they grow up. They allow us to live in their imagination—and their imagination becomes their solace, whence they can create worlds to escape in.'

'Like imaginary friends...' said Sharmeen.

'Yes. But we must draw that final curtain so that these children are forced to cope with the world. Their memory of us remains strong and manifests itself in their dreams. Do you understand what I am saying?'

Sharmeen nodded. 'Yes. You're letting me go, leaving me with a memory of you.'

Jugnu perched himself on the tip of her nose again. 'And you are not a little child, so you will never doubt that I ever existed. And there will be times when you will feel me near, and I will be, for I too am attached to my little human friend.'

Sharmeen reached out and touched the firefly on her nose gently. It glowed and the tip of her finger turned pink.

'Will you come if I am ever in trouble again, Jugnu?'

'Who knows what the future holds?'

Sharmeen nodded and dried her eyes with her knuckles. Her head hurt, as did her chest. 'I love you, Jugnu.'

'I love you too. Live well,' came the soft reply as Jugnu faded away.

Sharmeen stared at the gulmohar, its fiery flowers no longer lit by the soft glow of a firefly in the dark.

Acknowledgements

This book would not have been written had it not been for:

Afia Aslam who forced my unwilling ears to listen to the truly chilling true-to-life horror story that planted the seeds for this novel.

Ammi and Mahrukh, first readers, who declared that the book was good but I was weird.

Pooja Pande—my editor and literary humzaad.

Yusra Naqvi whose love, editing and excellent advice forced me out of my post-natal haze and made me finish the book.

Kanishka Gupta—agent and newest friend.

Aamer Hussein—friend, mentor and big brother in a strange new land.

Renuka Chatterjee who instantly believed in Sharmeen and her journey,

My daughter Sophia who reaffirmed my belief in magic.

And finally Asad Naqvi—husband, lover, critic and champion who never let me give up on myself.

www.ingramcontent.com/pod-product-compliance
Lightning Source LLC
Chambersburg PA
CBHW051105030726
47504CB00006B/1800